# FISTFUL OF FEET

## Jordan Krall

**Eraserhead Press**
Portland, OR

ERASERHEAD PRESS
205 NE BRYANT
PORTLAND, OR 97211

WWW.ERASERHEADPRESS.COM

ISBN: 1-933929-89-8

For my grandparents

# PART ONE
## Dig Your Grave......Calamaro is Coming

# CHAPTER ONE

The man named Calamaro walked across the Nevada desert, dragging a wooden donkey behind him. He pulled the donkey using leather reins that were wrapped around his wrists and palms. His flesh was already covered with burns from having dragged the donkey through the Dakota Territory and then into Nevada. It had been miles since Calamaro even felt the pain as his wrists and palms were simply numb.

He had been wandering for a while, not entirely sure where he was going, though in the back of his mind he had placed Screwhorse as his next destination. He had heard that there was gold to be found there. Even if he didn't find it, Calamaro knew that he could use the time to forget about his past.

The desert spread out before Calamaro like a hot, dusty carpet. He wasn't used to being in such a dry place. It made him think of the sea and the many hours he stood before it, staring at the horizon and basking in the sound of the waves as they lulled him into a meditative state. He missed the salt in the air and the sound of the waves as they hit the shore. Calamaro regretted ever having left New Jersey even though he had had no other choice.

Then he saw the town of Screwhorse on the horizon in all its dirty, dusty glory.

It had originally been a mining town but most of the mines were used up and those who didn't wish to leave stayed on to make Screwhorse a destination town for those who sought to indulge their more unique vices.

Calamaro dragged his donkey towards town and then saw the Indians. They had set up camp on the outskirts which was strange considering what he knew about the redskins. He also had no desire to come in contact with them as he was more than a bit frightened of their witchcraft. Most of his experiences with Indians had been weird ones and he had no desire to repeat those incidents.

The leather reins were digging into his wrists and palms but he kept at it, wanting to get to town as soon as possible. There was no use stopping until he had a comfortable place to rest. He walked in the opposite direction of the Indian camp and walked behind one of the buildings where there was a herd of cattle grazing on a tiny patch of desert grass.

Calamaro pulled his donkey close to the building, tied it to a wooden pole, and then walked past the cattle. He glanced at the animals and then one of them moved in close and bumped into him. Calamaro fell to the ground. More of the animals came closer until they were practically on top of him. He lifted himself up to his knees but was knocked down again. He looked up at the underbelly of one of the animals. Expecting to see udders, he saw something else.

Tentacles.

Thick, greenish-blue tentacles with tiny, wet suckers.

Calamaro got to his knees again and crawled away. He had seen cattle like that only once before when he was a boy and had snuck into a neighbor's farm. He had been trapped under the fishy-smelling cows for ten minutes but it had seemed like an eternity. It was not an experience he would like to repeat.

After crawling underneath two of the beasts, Calamaro stood up and walked to the front of the building. The words **HOTEL BRONSON** hung over the door in large black letters that had faded from the wind and dust.

Calamaro walked in and was greeted by a short man

with dozens of wrinkles that criss-crossed his face. The man nodded and said, "Hello."

"You have a room?"

The man nodded again. "I have ten of them."

"I just need one, Mr. Bronson."

"The name's Kersey, not Bronson. Mr. Bronson owns the place. I just work here. It'll be two dollars a night. Room is small but clean."

"That'll do." Calamaro dug into his pocket and then put the cash on the counter.

"Just a friendly warning. Sometimes strangers tend to come through here and want to start some trouble being that Screwhorse is just a small little town in the middle of nowhere. I recommend you not causing any problems. We got some tough boys in town who won't hesitate to give a stranger like yourself some trouble."

Calamaro gave Kersey a sly smile. "Trouble don't bother me none."

"You say so." He handed over the key. "Room's upstairs. Last one on the left."

Calamaro nodded. He started walking up the stairs but then stopped and turned his head. "I hope you don't mind I tied my animal to the post out back."

Kersey said, "I don't mind."

Calamaro went to his room and sat on the bed. He moved his head towards the window and closed his eyes. The sunlight lit up the inside of his eyelids.

He dozed off and quickly fell into a dream.

Calamaro was in a bank surrounded by naked women who were covered in green dust and red tattoos. They were busy making bricks and did not notice him as he walked around the room. He got to the vault and opened it, expecting to find the gold that he was looking for. The women stopped working and looked at Calamaro. He stared inside the vault.

There was no gold. Only corpses.

7

When Calamaro awoke, the first thing he saw was the faded floral wallpaper of the hotel room. The corpse vault and the naked women quickly leaked out of his consciousness. He stood up and walked out of the hotel room. It was time for a drink.

There was a combination bar and brothel across the street. There was a sign above the door that spelt out the name of the establishment in tall gaudy letters: **BETTY BLACK'S.**

From outside the door, Calamaro could hear the familiar sounds of a saloon and brothel. He walked in and the noise stopped.

Everyone turned and looked over. A black man near the door walked up to him and said in a smooth monotone voice, "Welcome to Betty Black's."

Calamaro said, "You greet everyone comes in the place?"

"Mostly everyone."

"I guess you probably make it a point to greet strangers, though." Calamaro smiled.

The black man grinned. "Can't argue with that."

"Not here for trouble. Just a drink or two."

"Then enjoy yourself."

Calamaro went up to the bar and ordered a whiskey. The barkeep was an older woman with gigantic freckled breasts that were practically popping out of her dress. She poured his drink and placed it in front of him.

"You want anything else? Some companionship maybe?"

Calamaro said, "No. Just a drink will do for now." He drank the shot. "You Betty Black?"

"Yes sir, I am." She leaned onto the bar, revealing more of her cleavage. "Why? You looking for me?"

"No, just wondering is all since that's the name of this place."

Betty nodded and walked down to the other end of the bar.

A group of men behind Calamaro were laughing loudly as they played cards. The loudest of the group, a huge bear of a man named Nix Morrow, was shouting at a skinny, bald man named Ryan Hickory.

"You sonovabitch!" Nix said. He flexed his muscles and flared his nostrils.

Ryan said, "What? What did I do?" He cackled.

"You're cheating," Nix said. "And why are you always laughing like a goddamn hyena?"

"I can't help it," Ryan said, laughing even harder now.

The third man at the table was young and short. He wore glasses and sat looking at his cards intently. Nix tapped the table and said, "Chaps, it's your turn."

Chaps took his glasses off and rubbed his nose. "I know, I know."

Nix said, "You're always so goddamn slow." He pointed at Ryan. "And this son of a bitch always cheats!"

Calamaro listened with amusement. The black man who greeted him walked over to the bar and asked, "How's your whiskey?"

"Fine as far as whiskey goes, I guess. Been in the desert so long I think my mouth is covered in dust so nothing tastes right."

"We don't water the shit down like they do in other places. Betty takes pride in her liquor."

"That's good to know," Calamaro said.

From behind them, Nix Morrow yelled, "Hey nigger!"

The black man turned his head. "You know my name. Feel free to use it."

Nix said, "You gonna give me orders? I think you forgot who you are. I think you should go look in a mirror. Remind yourself you're a nigger." Ryan laughed at his friend's remark. Chaps, on the other hand, was still staring at his cards.

Calamaro turned his head slightly and watched as the black man stood there, unfazed by the comments. There was confidence in the man that Calamaro had never really seen before in a Negro. Most of them that he had known seemed to keep their bravado buried deep. Calamaro said, "That asshole knows your name but I don't. What is it?"

"Stacklee."

Calamaro nodded.

Nix got louder. "Nigger, bring me a drink!"

Calamaro stared down at his empty shot glass and said, "You know the man's name. It might be nice if you used it." He made sure to say it loud enough so everyone in the place could hear.

At the table, Nix's eyes widened. He rarely had to deal with anyone challenging him.

Nix looked at Ryan. "You hear this? Some goddamn stranger walks in and starts protecting a nigger."

Ryan laughed.

Chaps stared at his cards. He knew it was his turn and that some ruckus was happening around him but he didn't care. He could not get yesterday's events out of his mind. Before he came to Screwhorse, he was known as the French Horn Kid on account of his always carrying the instrument around, playing it at inopportune times. But yesterday the horn was thrown out of the window by that whore Angie and then trampled by horses. That day was supposed to be special since he had just lost his virginity. Then the whore had to get all uppity on him because he asked if she'd be willing to lick the wet spot on the bed.

Chaps said, "What?"

"I said what's with this stranger sticking up for that nigger," Nix said.

"I don't know." All he could think of was his poor French horn.

Ryan laughed and said, "Maybe he likes dark meat."

At the bar, Calamaro was staring at his empty shot glass. Stacklee was looking at him. "You shouldn't have stuck your nose into this mess," he whispered.

Calamaro grunted.

Stacklee said, "I can handle these assholes myself."

"I'm sure you could. Still doesn't mean I enjoy listening to them."

Stacklee nodded. There was something about this stranger that he liked. Most of the drifters who passed through either ignored him or treated him like a slave. This man was different. "What's your name?"

"Calamaro."

From behind them, Nix exploded again. "Nigger!"

No one noticed that Calamaro had thrown the shot glass until it was practically lodged in Nix's eye socket. The asshole screamed and fell backwards off the chair. Ryan laughed but quickly changed it to a yell of anger. Chaps kept staring at his cards, thinking about his French horn.

Stacklee couldn't believe it. It happened so quickly. That bastard Nix was crying like a baby with a shot glass sticking out of his face.

"My eye! Shit!" Nix put his hands to his face. He pulled the glass out and threw it to the ground where it smashed.

Calamaro slowly got off the barstool. Betty Black stood behind the bar, shocked and confused at the turn of events. She was always used to those three assholes causing trouble but never was able to do anything considering that they worked for that bastard William Lyons. She had never witnessed anyone standing up to them except for Stacklee and even that went no further than a verbal confrontation.

She tugged on Calamaro's sleeve and said, "Just leave!" He ignored her.

Stacklee said, "She's right. You should leave." Calamaro ignored him, too. He walked over to Nix.

Ryan grabbed for his pistol but before he could take it out, Calamaro pulled his gun and pointed it at his crotch.

"Don't do anything you'll regret," Calamaro said.

Ryan stopped. He was not the brightest guy but he knew when he was outmatched. Besides, he didn't want his dick blown off. He put his pistol away.

Calamaro said, "You could've avoided this, you know." He put his gun back into its holster. "If there's one thing I hate, it's assholes."

Nix whimpered. "Fuck you."

Calamaro shook his head. "You might want to apologize to the man. I think you're aware his name's not nigger. He said you knew his name. I just learned it myself, actually. It's Stacklee. That refresh your memory? Do you want me to spell it for you?"

Blood dripping out of his eye, Nix said, "Fuck you."

"See, you talk to people like that, they might get the impression you're an asshole. Are you an asshole?" He wasn't worried about Ryan trying for his gun again. That guy was a coward if he had ever seen one.

Chaps finally looked up from his cards. "What the hell's happening here?"

"This your friend?" Calamaro said, pointing to Nix who was up on his knees, holding his eye.

"Yes sir, he's my friend. What's the problem?" Chaps said. Thoughts of his French horn were still floating around but now he was getting focused on Nix's bloody eye. "I didn't see him do anything to you so why'd you go and attack him?"

"Your friend doesn't know how to talk to people."

Ryan piped in. "What? Now you're sheriff around here, telling people what they can say?" He giggled. "Got a great idea. We can get the sheriff and tell him someone wants his job."

Nix stood up. He took his hand away from his eye, revealing a dark red and blue bruise. His eyeball was bloodshot and looked like it was pushed farther into his head than its twin. "You signed your death warrant, you know that? You come in, a stranger like you defending a goddamn nigger and attack a man who's just playing cards. That shows everyone what kind of man you are, know what I'm saying?"

Calamaro smiled. "For your sake, I hope you never

find out what kind of man I am."

From behind the bar, Betty Black laughed. She couldn't help it. She was amused by what could either be courage or stupidity on the part of the stranger.

Stacklee walked over and put his hand on Calamaro's shoulder. "It's okay. Let the men play their cards and leave. Shit's not gonna get any better if you all stand here seeing who has a bigger dick."

"Yeah, listen to the ni-," Nix said. He stopped himself and smiled. "Listen to Stacklee. He sure is a smart one, know what I'm saying?"

Calamaro nodded. He was done with the guy. Men like that never learned their lesson. It didn't matter whether Calamaro threw a whole whiskey bottle through his other eye, the guy would defend his manhood to the very end.

Stacklee touched his shoulder again. "Let's go."

Calamaro followed him back to the bar. He picked up a whiskey bottle and took a swig, looking at Betty Black. Then he said, "I'll pay for the bottle." He smiled. "And the shot glass."

# CHAPTER TWO

Once they were outside the brothel, Nix said, "You guys tell Lyons anything different and I'll smash your faces in, know what I'm saying?"

He had already come up with his version of the events. He'd tell William Lyons that they were sitting there playing cards when that stranger came in wanting to play the next hand. Nix refused and the stranger didn't take kindly to that. Nix told him to beat it but the guy just wouldn't go away. Then the stranger sucker-punched Nix in the eye and ran away like a yellow-bellied coward.

Ryan said, "You really think William's going to believe some guy just punched you and ran away? Why don't you just tell him we beat the shit out of the guy?"

"Because then he'll think it's over. It ain't over, know what I'm saying? I want us all to go after the man and I don't want Lyons telling me to back off. He's always telling me not to beat a dead horse. Well, I have to tell him the man hit me when I wasn't looking. Got it? You tell him anything different and you'll see what'll happen, you know what I'm saying?"

Ryan and Chaps nodded.

Nix said, "Chaps, you son of a bitch, you've been quiet tonight. What the hell's on your mind?"

"Nothing, boss," Chaps said. He was thinking of his French horn, thinking about it dancing in the moonlight and changing into a horse galloping on the horizon. He wanted to be

14

on that horse. He thought about riding it all the way to California to look for gold. Chaps thought about that goddamn whore who took both his virginity and destroyed his beloved instrument. Though he was filled with rage at the woman, he knew he would never do anything about it. Instead, he would wallow in self-pity until he got himself another French horn. His thoughts were interrupted by Nix punching him in the shoulder.

Ryan laughed as Chaps almost fell over from the blow.

Nix said, "Both you assholes better get the story straight or else, know what I'm saying?"

"Sure thing, boss," Ryan said.

Nix grunted and watched as a stagecoach rode down the street. He always loved when a new batch of people came into town. It gave him the chance to recruit someone into his fold or at least give him the chance to show off. As the stagecoach stopped in front of the hotel, Nix made sure to stand up straight and flex his muscles. If there were any ladies on board, he wanted them to see his manly physique. Then he remembered his black eye. There was no way he wanted anyone to see that.

Nix quickly turned around and started walking. "What're you jackasses waiting for? Let's go see Lyons."

# CHAPTER THREE

Rebecca Bywater looked out the stagecoach window and sighed.

It wasn't that she wanted to be a whore. It's not like she woke up one day and decided that getting screwed by dirty men was her destiny. She just figured it was the quickest way to get the money she needed to move to California.

Her cousin had told her about a town in Nevada called Screwhorse and how the brothel there was one of the most lucrative in the state. Men would pay good money for some weird things and some of those things weren't even that difficult. Some men wanted to be spit on, some wanted to suck toes, and some men just wanted to smell a woman's armpits. Rebecca didn't think any of that would be bad at all.

So there she was on a stagecoach from Phoenix, making her way into Screwhorse. Rebecca had seen a tribe of Indians on the way in and that made her a little bit nervous as she'd never had any good experiences with redskins. She always thought they were looking at her strangely, as if secretly wishing that they could roast her over a fire during one of their pagan rituals. At least she'd be protected in town, she thought. There was no way that the law didn't offer protection against the possibility of attack.

Her first stop would be **BETTY BLACK'S**, the brothel. From what Rebecca had heard, the woman who runs it looks out for her girls and provides them with a clean place to live.

Out of the corner of her eye, Rebecca saw that the man

16

sitting across from her was staring at her again. He had done it practically the whole trip. She didn't mind all that much. The man was attractive enough though he was dressed strange, all fancy like a stuffy Englishman.

When the stagecoach finally stopped, Rebecca quickly got off and put some distance between her and the man. She walked to the brothel, walked inside, and put down her suitcase. It wasn't what she had expected. There weren't naked women dancing all over the tables like she had imagined. In fact, the place was pretty classy for a brothel.

A black man by the bar walked over and greeted her with a small smile. "Help you, miss?" he said. "You lost?"

Rebecca didn't smile back at the man. It wasn't that she really hated Negroes but she grew up with a mild fear of them due to all the stories her father had told her about how they treated white women. She said, "No, I'm not lost. I'm looking for the lady who runs this establishment."

"Then you're looking for Betty. That's her over there behind the bar. Want me to hold your bag for you?"

Rebecca quickly grabbed the handle of her suitcase and said, "No, thank you."

The black man shrugged and walked away.

Behind the bar was a woman who was old enough to be Rebecca's mother but lively enough to be a younger sister. She was pouring drinks for two very tall and very filthy men.

Walking with her head held high, Rebecca approached the bar and said, "Excuse me. Betty?"

The woman said, "Yeah, I'm Betty." She looked down at the suitcase. "If you want the hotel, it's across the street."

"No, I don't want a hotel. Can we talk in private?"

Betty nodded. She looked over Rebecca's shoulder at the black man. "Stacklee, watch the bar, will you?"

"Sure thing," Stacklee said.

Betty brought Rebecca to a back room. She motioned to a couch. "Have a seat."

"Thank you." Rebecca sat down, making sure she sat prim and proper. After all, she didn't want the woman to think she was just some common street whore.

"What can I do for you?" Betty said.

"I'd like to work here. In your establishment."

Betty laughed. "Honey, you know how many girls have said that over the years? You know how many have begged to work here and then ran out two days later after some crusty old miner asked her to sneeze on his pecker? To earn your money you have to be willing to do more than just lie on your back and stare at the ceiling. This ain't a picnic, you know. It's not like one of those brothels back east. I have no room for lazy whores."

"I'm sure you don't. I need employment and I am willing and able to fulfill the requirements. I've heard about this place. I know what goes on here."

"You do, do you?"

"Yes, I do. I'm not just some farmer's daughter who doesn't know about the world. I have goals, too."

"Such as?"

"I plan to make enough money to get to California and start a life there. Have a husband. Have children. To do that, I'm prepared to do whatever it takes even if that includes sneezing on a couple of dirty peckers."

Betty leaned over and patted Rebecca's hand. "That's good you want to get married but you know most men don't want to marry a whore."

"Are you saying I can't work here?"

"I didn't say that. I'm just trying to give you a chance to see clearly so that you don't end up blaming me for anything that happens later on."

Rebecca frowned. "I never blame anyone for my problems."

"That's good," Betty said. "Still, I'd like to think about it. Until then, you can stay here. You'll have to pay for the room until I make up my mind. After that, your food and lodging comes out of your earnings. Understand?"

"Yes. Thank you."

"Go talk to Stacklee and he'll take you to the room. He's the one who greeted you when you came in."

Rebecca's eyes widened. "May I ask what he's here for? It's a little strange seeing a Negro working in a place like this. Should I be worried?"

"If you have any problems with Negroes you best get rid of them before you even think about working here. Stacklee's here to protect the girls and he works with me just as if he was a white man. He's like family. You don't have to worry about him."

"If you say so," Rebecca said. She wasn't entirely at ease but knew that if she said any more about it, Betty would definitely decide against offering her the job. So she went out front and asked Stacklee if he'd take her to the empty room. He obliged and brought her up the stairs.

When she walked into the room, the first thing Rebecca noticed was the stains on the walls. She could only imagine where they came from but she knew that inquiring about them wouldn't be in her best interest if she wanted employment. It never paid to be too critical.

After putting her suitcase on the bed, Rebecca sat down next to it. She looked at the streaks on the wall in front of her and thought one of them looked like blood. Was it safe staying here?

Though she never considered herself a religious woman, she hoped to God that she wouldn't be in danger. Rebecca had practically given up on any sort of religion after that reverend back in Phoenix had tried to rape her in the name of the Lord. Though she managed to get away without being violated, she lost all faith in religion and in so-called holy men in general.

Rebecca sat in the chair by the window. The stagecoach ride had been tiring and she wanted nothing more than to relax for a few minutes after which she'd try to impress Betty by flirting with some customers. She looked out the window at the town below. Though it had all the qualities of every other western town she'd seen, there was something strange about Screwhorse. Rebecca couldn't readily identify it but it tugged at her gut like bad whiskey. Maybe coming here wasn't such a good idea, she thought.

\* \* \*

On the stagecoach ride, Bluford Barnes had tried his best to hide his erection but that woman was just too damn arousing. He had stolen glances at her whenever he could get away with it. When he wasn't looking at her face or her cleavage, he snuck glances at her dirty boots. He imagined himself underneath them, the heel of it digging into his forehead.

He thought that it was dangerous for a woman to ride unescorted for such a long way. Though he considered himself a gentleman who would never hurt a lady, Bluford understood how some men might take an opportunity like that to get themselves some pussy.

So Bluford didn't make any move to talk to the lady since he knew that she was probably unescorted for a reason. Maybe she knew how to handle herself pretty damn well and had a revolver hidden somewhere on her, cocked and ready to blow a hole through any man who tried to get fresh. Bluford wasn't about to risk his life just to relieve his erection. No sir. Instead, he decided that he'd get it taken care of when he reached Screwhorse. The whores there were supposed to be top-notch. He had heard that there was one lady who could spit whiskey out of her cunny and right into your mouth. That amazed Bluford. They didn't have women like that back east.

When they finally reached Screwhorse, he let the lady get out first and then he stepped down off the stagecoach with his suitcase in front of his crotch. He saw the woman walk in the direction of **BETTY BLACK'S** and then thought that maybe she was a whore. If he'd only gotten the courage to talk to her on the ride over, she might've thrown him a free one. Shit, it was just his luck riding all those miles with a woman like that without even knowing it.

Bluford had more urgent plans, though. He had to get a room and then scope out the town. He knew that many of the citizens were supposedly pretty tough but figured he could probably swindle a few of them out of some cash before he moved on to the next town. After all, that was his area of expertise, wasn't it? The Barnes clan had spent years honing their craft and they passed on that knowledge to Bluford who turned out to be the most successful confidence man in the family. He hustled and schemed his way through all of the towns he'd been through with no problem at all.

With a spring in his step, Bluford walked over to the hotel, making sure to greet everyone who crossed his path. He found that most townspeople are suspicious of strangers unless they're friendly and outgoing. The women especially warmed up to polite, clean-shaven young men and so that's who he became: a handsome charmer. He had spent a lot of money on his suits, buying them from an English tailor in New York City. Appearance was everything and dressing fancy was what allowed Bluford to get far in his occupation as a cheat.

As he made his way down Main Street, Bluford walked by a short man with a bald head. His skin had an orange tint and his teeth were too big for his mouth. The man said, "Hey you."

"Yes, sir?" Bluford stopped and smiled.

"See that motherfucker over there?"

"I'm sorry?"

The man pointed across the street. "See that motherfucker?"

Bluford politely shook his head. "I'm sorry, sir. All I see is a horse."

"That's the motherfucker I'm talking about. See him?"

"Uh, yes."

"You know what nerve that motherfucker had? He

21

was talking about me again, spreading rumors."

Bluford slowly took a step but stopped when he saw the man raise his fist.

"You going somewhere?" the man said. "And why the hell you dressed like that?"

"Dressed like what, sir? I don't understand."

"All clean and fancy like you're one of those pretty boys from England. You from England?"

"No, sir," Bluford said. "But if you'll excuse me, I do have to leave."

"Then get the hell out of here." The bald man turned and looked at the horse across the street. "Yeah, that's right, motherfucker! I'm talking about you!"

Bluford quickly walked away and went into the hotel. At first sight, he wasn't that impressed with it. He was used to finer accommodations. Still, he wasn't about to make a fuss about it since the purpose of his visit to Screwhorse was not relaxation. He was there to work.

Looking at the man behind the counter, Bluford said, "Hello, sir. I'd like to arrange for some lodging."

Kersey nodded.

As Bluford signed the register, he said, "Is this the only hotel in town?"

"Afraid so. Why?"

Bluford smiled. "Oh, no reason, sir."

"You want to stay here or not?"

"Oh yes sir, I certainly do," Bluford said. "I do have a question, though. There was a man outside, seemed like something was wrong with him. He was threatening a horse. Should the sheriff be notified?"

Kersey's face turned pale. "That's the Hard Candy Kid. You best stay away from him."

Bluford nodded. "That little man a bully, then?"

"Don't let his size fool you," Kersey said. "He's a killer."

"Oh," Bluford said. "Well then," He cleared his throat. He was glad that he hadn't given the Hard Candy Kid a difficult time.

Kersey said, "One piece of advice. You might want to pick up some sucking candy from the General Store. Next time you run into the Hard Candy Kid, just give him a piece and he'll be more likely to leave you be."

"Thank you. I'll look into that." Bluford went up to his room. He wasn't impressed with that either. There were huge stains in the rug as well as on the walls. It wasn't worth making a fuss about it. That would just attract the wrong kind of attention.

He unpacked his bags, took out his gear, and headed off to **BETTY BLACK'S**. It was time to get to work.

\* \* \*

Unknown to Bluford Barnes and Rebecca Bywater, someone was watching them from afar. It was someone who felt flushed with rage when Rebecca walked into the brothel and when Bluford tried unsuccessfully to cover his erection.

One of them would have to die. The woman could be cut or drowned. She could be made to lick her own boots, spitting and drooling until they were completely covered in thick slop. Then she could be made to choke on her own boot leather, the foot stench filling her nostrils until her last breath was gone.

The man could be stabbed and drowned in piss. He could be humiliated and tortured. He could be made to eat desert sand until his ass burned and bled.

Someone was watching with glee, thinking about Rebecca's breasts being sliced open and left there for the scorpions.

Someone was giggling, savoring the thought of seeing the man beg as his torture increased.

That someone was a killer.

And the killer would kill again.

# CHAPTER FOUR

When Calamaro reached for his money, Stacklee pushed his hand away.

"I'll take care of it," he said. "As much as I think you did a dumb thing, I do appreciate it. Least I can do is pay for your drink while you're still breathing."

"Guys didn't seem so tough."

"It's not those guys you should be worried about. It's William Lyons, the man they work for."

Calamaro shrugged. "That name supposed to mean something?"

"He's made a name for himself over the years mainly for being a cold son of a bitch. He was in the army. Killed lots of Indians, Mexicans, and basically anyone else ain't like him."

"But he leaves you alone?"

"He pretty much just ignores me. I'm just a dumb nigger to him, I guess. Lyons ain't going to just walk up to a black man and shoot him. He wouldn't want to waste a bullet. He'd feel it was like stomping on a bug. It wouldn't be worth his time."

Calamaro sipped his whiskey and savored it. "What happened tonight, would that be a good reason for him to stomp on you?"

"Don't know. I've messed with those boys before and Lyons doesn't seem to care all that much probably on account of them being dumb as shit, figure they can't help but piss people off. What's he going to do, kill everyone who doesn't get along with those guys? He'd have to kill everyone in town."

24

"I'd still keep my eyes open, I was you."

"I always do," Stacklee said. "But don't get the wrong idea. This town is full of good people even though our mayor is a son of a bitch. And then there's the Hard Candy Kid. He's one to stay away from. Even William Lyons has enough sense to tread lightly around him."

Calamaro nodded. "Sounds to me like this town is full of tough guys."

"Maybe so," Stacklee said. He knocked on the bar. "Hey Betty, come give us another bottle, will you?"

Betty said, "Sure thing, Stack." She set down a fresh bottle of whiskey in front of them. She locked her eyes on Calamaro's. "Listen....what was your name again?"

"Calamaro."

"Calamaro what?"

"Just Calamaro."

"Listen, Calamaro," Betty said. "I appreciate what you did for Stacklee. He's a good friend and a good worker. But you're not from around here. You don't know this town or the people in it. It was mighty stupid of you to get involved. Stacklee here could've handled himself."

"I know that. I didn't do it because I thought the man needed protecting. I did it because I've no patience for assholes who run their mouths."

Betty laughed. "Fair enough, fair enough."

One of her girls walked downstairs and told Betty that Mary wanted to speak to her.

"Mind watching the bar, Stack?"

"Sure thing," Stacklee said. "You mind if I put our new friend to work? Maybe he can sweep the floor or something."

Betty winked. "If you can get him to do it, go ahead."

"I haven't swept a floor in years so I can't promise you I'll do a good job," Calamaro said, smiling.

Stacklee laughed and patted the stranger on the shoulder. "Don't worry, I'll teach you all you need to know."

# CHAPTER FIVE

Mayor Douglas lived in a two story building just outside of Screwhorse. Many of the townspeople criticized the fact that the mayor didn't live in town but none were brave enough to actually voice their grievances publicly. Therefore, Mayor Douglas was able to peacefully go about his business which mainly consisted of drinking expensive liquor and screwing his Mexican whore, Ana.

When he had acquired Ana, Mayor Douglas planned on her simply being a silent fuck toy. Much to his dismay she proved to be an ambitious little slut who was as manipulative as she was a good screw.

Mayor Douglas heard the hidden door in the wall open and saw Ana walk in. She was wearing only a skirt and was dragging a naked woman by the hair. The woman was olive skinned and the mayor figured she was probably one of those Italians he kept hearing about. He always told his men to nab any good looking bitch they came across. If anyone had a problem with it, then they were instructed to kill even if that meant exterminating a whole family. Atrocities could always be blamed on Indians.

Ana brought the woman over to the mayor. She squeezed one of the woman's breasts until it resembled a purple sack of jelly. The woman cried out and was answered by Ana's hand as it slapped her face. "Tell the mayor your name."

The woman looked up fearfully and said, "Belladonna."

Ana slapped her again. "Belladonna what?"

"Belladonna Cardinale."

Mayor Douglas looked closer at the woman and saw that her back was covered in red tattoos. That intrigued him and he knew he'd have fun looking at them while he screwed her from behind.

"Miss Cardinale, I'm the mayor of this town. Do you know what that means?"

The woman shook her head. "No."

"It means I can do any goddamn thing I want to do. If I want to make you my footstool, I will. If I want to make you lie on the floor while Ana here pisses all over you, I will. Do you understand what I'm telling you?"

The woman nodded. "Yes."

"For now I'm content to make you lean over my desk so I can poke that cute Italian pussy of yours. Maybe your ass, too. You ever been fucked in the ass? No, I don't expect you would have. A lot of men don't like it but the way I figure it, a little shit on a man's pecker never hurt anybody." He pointed to his trousers and Ana walked over and unbuckled them for him. She reached in and pulled out his small penis.

He said, "So, Belladonna Cardinale, stand up, bend over, and take it like a good whore."

For the next fifteen minutes, Belladonna Cardinale endured the mayor's mushroom-cap penis plunging inside her while Ana watched, cackling like a witch. She was always happy watching a weak woman get dominated. It reminded Ana of her younger self and all the pain she had to endure by the hands of her father and brothers. Because of that, she vowed never to be weak again.

"Fuck her good," Ana said, moving her fingers down to her crotch. "Fuck her until she's bleeding." She was disappointed when the mayor yelped and stopped his screwing. He wiped his brow with his forearm.

"Get the hell out of my sight," he said to Belladonna.

27

She quickly moved away from him and went back through the hidden door.

Ana smiled and said, "So how was she?"

"I was talking to you, too, whore. Get the hell out of my sight," Mayor Douglas said.

Her smile turning into an angry frown, Ana turned abruptly and followed Belladonna through the door in the wall. She slammed it shut.

Mayor Douglas was left alone in his office. He looked down at his penis and saw that it was now covered in the same intricate tattoos that had adorned Belladonna's back.

He spat on his palm and rubbed. The tattoos wouldn't come off.

"Those fucking Italians," he said, moving his lit cigar towards his penis.

'

# CHAPTER SIX

Betty Black had been running the brothel ever since Screwhorse became a town. She prided herself on running a classy place. There were no smelly, toothless whores here like they had in the other mining towns. No sir, all of her whores were clean, pretty, and almost always whole.

She walked up the stairs, wondering what the hell Mary wanted. Usually the girls took care of business themselves without having to bother Betty with the details. She loved the girls and would do anything for them but Betty just liked it better when she wasn't being whined to about the customers.

"Betty," Mary said. "Timothy Horn's here again."

"I know. I saw him go up with you. What's the matter?"

"I'm not sure I'm keen on doing what he wants."

Betty rolled her eyes. "Honey, what do I tell you girls? If you don't want to do something, then just find another girl who will."

"I know, I know. Thing is, I already offered to get him another girl and he says that he won't leave until I do it, no one else. He said I remind him of a girl he once knew. Trust me, if it was any other man you know I'd get Stacklee to throw him out."

"And we can't do that. Then we'd have his uncle closing us down," Betty said. She hated when the mayor's nephew came in. It wasn't that he was so much trouble. There are days when he was a perfect gentleman. It was just that he was just so goddamn crazy. There was something seriously wrong with the boy.

Mary said, "Well, I don't know what to do."

"What's he want? Don't say he wants you to take a shit on him. I know you've done that before."

"No, it's not that. That don't bother me none," Mary said. "He has some sort of dead animal, something from the ocean or something, has a bunch of legs. Really ugly. He wants me to put it under the bed while we fuck."

"And?"

"That's it! He wants me to leave the thing under the bed while we do it. Thing smells like shit! I'm not letting him put some dead smelly thing there. What if the smell don't go away?"

"I don't see the big deal, hon. Let him put it under the bed, stuff some cotton up your nose, let him have a poke at you, and then just make sure he takes the damn thing out when he leaves."

"I just don't feel right about it, Betty. I can't stand the smell of the thing. You want to come in and take a whiff?"

"No, I don't." Betty put up her hands. "Mary, do what you think is best. But let me tell you something. That boy better come out of that room a happy little bastard. Understand?"

"Yeah," Mary said. She turned and sulked back to her room. Betty shook her head. Mary was a good girl and Betty felt bad making her do something she didn't want to do but it wasn't that odd considering a lot of the other requests they'd received. Besides, Timothy Horn had to leave satisfied. If he did, then his uncle was satisfied and that meant no trouble for the brothel.

\* \* \*

When Mary got to the door, she opened it slowly and peeked in. There he was sitting on the edge of the bed with the dead animal on his lap, tentacles drooping down his legs and onto the floor. It was already starting to stink up the room.

She knew Betty was right and that it would be better for all of them if Timothy Horn left satisfied but she just couldn't stand it. It wasn't just the smell. Just the thought of screwing around when that thing was underneath the bed made her crazy.

Mary walked in, closed the door behind her, and said, "Okay, sweetie. Let's get this over with."

Timothy stood up and smiled. "Change of plans."

Mary listened as Timothy Horn explained what he wanted to do instead of putting that ugly creature under the bed while they fucked. She hated to admit it but Betty was right. That crazy prick Timothy had to leave a happy man. That still didn't make her any more comfortable with what he had planned.

He said, "See what we're going to do, we're going to pretend this here is Lincoln and you're going to be Lincoln's wife. You're going to sit next to him here." He patted the bed where he had laid the dead animal down on the quilt. "Now, I'm going to be the assassin, see, and I'm going to shoot him." He smiled. "Let me ask you, do you know where Lincoln was killed?"

Mary said, "Was a theatre, right?"

"Yes. Good girl, good girl. It was a theatre but we're going to do it differently, see. We're going to make believe we're in an open-topped stagecoach and I'm going to be over there on the other side of the room making believe I'm hiding behind a fence or a bush or something."

"You know you can't shoot your gun in here. Betty'll have a fit."

"I'm not going to use a gun, Mary," he said. "So just come and have a seat on the bed next to the President here while I go prepare for the assassination." Timothy got undressed and walked over to the corner. He crouched down and gestured for Mary to sit on the bed next to the creature.

Mary looked at the thing and felt bile rise into her mouth. It was such an ugly animal: dark pink and slimy with all those legs draped over the bed. It reminded her of the time she and another prostitute had explored each other's pussies.

31

Everything was so weird and wet. That experience had been disgusting and arousing at the same time. How can something so ugly like a pussy cause so much pleasure? Mary wondered if it was going to be the same type of experience.

She pointed to the creature. "Wait, what the hell is that thing, anyway?"

"Called a squid. My uncle got it from a friend of his who lives back east. New Jersey, actually. That's where my family came from originally."

"Is that what passes for a pet? They don't have dogs in New Jersey?"

"Don't know. This guy my uncle knows, he's a judge over there, name's Judge Kinski, maybe you've heard of him?"

Mary shook her head.

"Anyway, Judge Kinski liked to walk along the beaches there and one time he came across an Indian who was sitting with this thing on the beach, holding it like a baby. The judge asked the redskin what the hell he was doing and you know what the redskin said?"

Mary shook her head again.

"He said that he was trying to wake up some sort of god that lives in the sea. Those Indians are pagans, you know, devil worshippers."

"So that judge decided to just take this squid thing?"

"Yeah. After he shot the Indian, that is. Shot him right in the mouth. He said there were teeth everywhere. I think he even gathered a few of them up, too. My uncle said the judge took those teeth and made them into dentures. I think he gave a few to my uncle, too."

She rolled her eyes. "That judge sounds like a real nice fellow."

Timothy Horn stood up from his crouch, stretched, and then went back into position. "So are you ready?"

"Guess so." She sat next to the creature and hung her feet off the bed. "What do you want me to do exactly?"

32

"I'm going to assassinate the bastard and you just go on screaming like if it was your husband being shot dead right in front of you. You can imagine what that'd be like, can't you? Pieces of his brains and skull all over the place and you just get all crazy and shocked so you try to pick up the pieces."

"That's sickening," Mary said.

"If it makes you sick, that's alright. I imagine if you really saw your husband get shot in front of you that you'd probably vomit anyway. Just go with it, Mary. Lord knows I'm paying you enough. Now just sit right there and look at that wall and pretend you're just enjoying the carriage ride."

Mary did what she was told. She sat next to the smelly Lincoln-creature and stared at the wall. Out of the corner of her eye she saw Timothy touching himself. Then he said, "Okay, now make believe you see someone you know out there yonder. Wave to them and keep waving until I tell you to stop."

She waved reluctantly. It was a strange thing to do but Mary had to admit that waving was preferable to some of the other requests she had come across like Doctor West who had wanted to perform extremely invasive medical examinations with bizarre equipment made of glass and bone. She had staunchly refused every time yet the doctor came back week after week with the same request.

Her daydream was interrupted by Timothy saying, "Bang, bang, you're dead! Bang, bang, you're dead!" He tiptoed to the bed and starting sticking his index finger into the squid and then continued to stick all of his fingers in, scooping out stringy pieces of flesh. Mary jumped off the bed.

"Holy shit!" She stood with her back against the farthest wall in the room.

Timothy looked at her. "That's it! Keep going! Scream to high heaven! Look! Your husband's brains are everywhere! Everywhere!"

Mary closed her eyes. She didn't want to watch him mutilate the squid with his fingers even if the thing was already dead. She could hear the squishy sounds of Timothy's hand as it went in and out of the wet carcass.

"Mary! Come here and gather up some of your husband's brains and skull! Come on! Your president needs you!"

"No! Just stop!" she said. "Stop before I call Stacklee!"

The noise stopped. Mary opened her eyes and saw Timothy standing there naked, covered in squid juice and squid flesh. He didn't look happy.

"I paid you to do something for me and I expect it to be done, see? You have the nerve to threaten me with calling your damned nigger friend? What's he going to do about it?"

Maybe it was the fact that she was being yelled at or the sight of Timothy covered in putrid slop but whatever it was, it made her want to fall down to the floor and weep. So that's what she did.

Timothy sighed heavily. "Mary, don't cry. I'm sorry I yelled. You have to understand I just get angry sometimes." He walked over to her and put his hand on her cheek. "Just come back over to the bed and pick up some of the pieces, okay?"

Mary couldn't believe that the man went from yelling to apologizing and then back to insisting that she follow through with what got her upset in the first place. But she thought of what Betty had told her. Timothy Horn must leave satisfied.

"Okay," said Mary, looking at the floor. She walked over to the bed and started picking up pieces of squid flesh with her right hand and putting them into her left. Timothy stood behind her touching himself.

"That's it, Mary. If you feel like crying again, don't hold it in."

She let tears flow but not because Timothy wanted her to but because if she didn't, she was sure she'd end up feeling worse. After a minute Mary had a handful of the creature's flesh. Then she felt Timothy's penis against her leg.

"You know, Mary. I'm paying you for two days. You're to stay with me all night. We may have to do this a few times to get it right. The president can be mighty finicky."

Mary sighed and said, "Okay."

"Now let's see if you can milk me like a cow," he said.

Mary was afraid to turn around but did anyway. After all, she had to make sure Timothy Horn left a happy man.

# CHAPTER SEVEN

Leonard Garko was relieved when they finally reached Screwhorse. He was exhausted and he knew that Sergio and Clayton were, too. Because of lack of water, their horses had been unable to go on. Leonard, Sergio, and Clayton left the animals and continued on foot. So once they got there, the town was a sight for sore eyes.

"Let's go over there," Leonard said. "The brothel." He thought it was a good idea to get a drink or two. There'd be pussy, too, but Leonard was planning to only quench his thirst, not his lust. He'd leave the whores to his younger partners, Sergio and Clayton.

They had traveled a long way to find the gold and Leonard didn't think it'd hurt if they took time to blow off some steam. Sergio had gotten more melancholy each day so any diversion might be for the better. After all, coming to the town was Sergio's idea to begin with and if he wasn't in the right mind, the whole plan would go to shit.

The only thing that bothered Leonard was that Clayton was wearing the donkey mask again. The guy went from putting it on occasionally to wearing the thing every single day without taking it off even to sleep. Leonard thought it was the stupidest thing he'd ever seen but didn't bother to voice his opinion since Sergio didn't seem to mind.

As they walked down Main Street, they passed the Hard Candy Kid who was yelling at a horse, slapping it across the face. Clayton laughed. "Look at that son of a bitch."

The Hard Candy Kid turned around, his eyes burning.

For a few seconds, Clayton and the Kid stared at each other until Sergio and Leonard walked into the brothel. At that point, Clayton nodded and said, "Asshole."

The Hard Candy Kid looked at the horse. "Motherfucker's wearing a mask, you see that? So ugly he has to cover up his face."

"Fuck you say?" Clayton said.

In a high, mocking voice, the Hard Candy Kid said, "Fuck you say? Fuck you say?" He opened his mouth and sent his face into the side of the horse, biting the animal until he had a mouthful of flesh and hair.

Clayton took a few steps back. "What the hell is wrong with you?"

"Wrong?" the Hard Candy Kid said, spitting the gore out of his mouth. He pulled a pistol from his waistband and pointed it at Clayton's face. "You're the one wearing a mask, asshole."

Clayton froze. He hadn't even seen a weapon on the guy. The son of a bitch was fast. "I don't want trouble," he said. He suddenly felt a deluge of sweat underneath his donkey mask.

"Trouble?" The Hard Candy Kid laughed. "You know what real trouble is? Real trouble is being shot and waking up to find yourself in Hell." With his free hand, he pointed to the horse. "Hell is paved with horse flesh, you know." He holstered his gun.

Clayton considered himself a tough son of a bitch but he was smart enough to know when he was outmatched. Besides, he had come into town with a goal in mind and starting trouble with a crazy horse-biter wasn't going to make things go any smoother. He slowly walked away from the Hard Candy Kid, following his friends into the brothel.

# CHAPTER EIGHT

Betty decided to check on June who had been sick for the last week. It was a shame losing out on seven days of income. That girl brought in a lot of money. Plenty of cowhands who passed through Screwhorse loved taking a poke at a girl with four feet. Of course two of those feet were tiny and grew out of June's ankles but the men still found it irresistible.

She knocked on the door. "June, honey? You alright? Can I come in?"

A childlike voice said, "Yes."

When Betty walked in, she saw June on the floor, naked and shivering. Her bedpan was next to her and it was filled with dark blue vomit.

"Oh my god! June!" She rushed over, grabbed a blanket from the bed, and covered the girl. "Why didn't you yell for one of us? Look at you!"

June said, "I don't feel all that bad."

"What about this?" Betty pointed to the bedpan. "You must've got rid of your dinner for the last week. Let's get you into bed and then I'll fetch Doctor West."

"No," June said. "I'm fine. Don't call the doctor. I just need some sleep is all. I'm just really tired." She let Betty help her into bed. "Thank you."

"Now you get some shuteye, sweetie."

"I will. But not until you tell me about the stranger downstairs."

"How'd you hear about him?"

June smirked. "Oh, I might've been spying."

"And you wonder why you're not getting better, moving around when you know damn well you're supposed to be in bed."

"You're not my momma, Betty, even though you're old enough to be." She giggled and then coughed, clearing her throat of thick phlegm. "So, tell me about the stranger."

Betty smiled. "What? There's nothing to tell. He came in and got mixed up with Nix and his boys. They were bothering Stacklee."

"That stranger better watch out. William Lyons won't be happy," June said.

"I know, I know. But you should've seen him, the stranger. He threw a glass right at Nix's eye. It was beautiful as much as it was funny."

"So what's his name?"

"Calamaro."

"Where's he from?"

"I don't know. I didn't ask him." Betty got up from the bed. "You need your sleep. Stop worrying about handsome strangers and worry about getting well."

June giggled. "So you think he's handsome?"

"Oh, don't be silly. I'm old enough to be his mother, too. Go to sleep," Betty said, walking out of the room while trying to hide her smile. She didn't mean to let it slip, her thinking the stranger was handsome. It was a long time since she had been attracted to a man in that way. After seeing all the dirty bastards coming in and out of the brothel, it was hard seeing a man as anything more than a customer.

Still, was there anything wrong with her thinking the stranger was good-looking? After all, she was still a woman. It wasn't like she was going to pursue him. That would just be damned silly. Betty walked slowly down the stairs, fixing her hair on the way down.

* * *

As soon as Betty left, June jumped out of bed. She walked to the door and opened it an inch. When the hallway was clear, she opened the door wider and tip-toed to the next room.

She opened the door and walked in.

On the wall was a starfish the size of a dinner plate. It was dark green with small yellow dots. Against the floral wallpaper, it created a focal point that was both disturbing and fascinating. At least this was the case for June who had taken every opportunity to sneak into the room to stare at the thing.

June didn't know how it got there and was more than a little afraid that it had something to do with her sickness. She didn't care, though. She was starting to love the creature.

"Hey you," she said to the starfish as it slowly slid down the wallpaper. June knew it wouldn't talk back but she hoped that it understood her just like horses understood. But was this thing as smart as a horse? June thought that maybe the thing was even smarter. After all, it found its way into this room. An animal must be pretty clever to do such a thing.

As soon as she spoke, the starfish stopped moving.

June smiled. "You didn't have to stop," she told it.

The starfish started sliding down the wall again but this time it moved slower than before.

"You want me to bring you to my room?"

It stopped again. June took that to mean that the creature didn't want to leave. But maybe it was telling her to take it back to her room, back to her warm bed so they could snuggle together as woman and starfish. Just to be on the safe side, June decided not to move it.

She said, "Don't you worry, I'm not bringing you anywhere."

The starfish continued sliding down the wall. As it did so, it left a trail of translucent slime.

"You're cute, you know that?" She wanted to touch it.

She wanted to pick it up like a baby and hug it, kiss it, tell it that she would be there for it no matter what.

June wanted to be a mother. She wanted to be the mother that she herself never knew. When she was born, her parents took one look at her two extra feet and left her for dead in a field outside of Newark, New Jersey.

So as June stared at the starfish on the wall, she felt a longing to breastfeed it. Of course she knew she wasn't nursing and that the very act of it was impossible but that still didn't deter the desire to nourish the creature with her mammary glands. She also wanted to wrap it in a blanket and take it for a walk. If anyone asked to see the "baby", she could just say that it was sick and couldn't be near anyone but its mother. Yes, that's what she could do.

June stepped closer to the creature. Her hand slowly moved towards it and that's when she was hit with a stab of nausea. It brought her down to her knees. June was now sure that her current illness had something to do with the creature.

Drowsiness set in quickly. As she stared at the wallpaper directly below the starfish, red and blue starbursts bombarded her until the whole room exploded in liquid color. The starfish was at the center and now it had a face. June turned away from it as if it was the very face of God and to simply catch a glimpse of it would mean damnation or insanity.

She looked down at her body and saw that she only had two feet. The two extra that had grown out of her ankles were gone. A feeling of relief shuddered through her. Maybe the first twenty-three years of her life were really just one long dream. Maybe she was just a normal two-footed girl with loving parents who would laugh when she told them her terribly absurd dream about having four feet. They'd say, "That's just ridiculous, sweetie. No one has four feet."

June started to walk but stumbled onto the floor and landed on her back, making a splash into an iridescent pile of gooey light. She looked down and saw that she still had four feet. The starfish was now above her and was lowering itself with what looked like a pink spider web. It dropped onto her chest and lifted itself up on two legs. She covered her eyes and said, "Don't scare your mother."

She felt it latch onto her left breast.

It started to suckle.

June felt a strange sensation, the sensation of milk being drawn from her breast by the mouth of a starfish. It wasn't unpleasant.

"You must be hungry," she said, uncovering her eyes and looking down at the creature. It had grown to twice its original size. June surrendered to the strange, wet creature suckling at her tit. She surrendered to the swirling colors that enveloped the room. But most of all she surrendered to the feeling that she finally was able to be involved in a nurturing mother-child relationship. It was a strange one, yes, but it was at least something that she had never experienced before and that made her feel good.

June still could not look directly at the starfish because she didn't want to see its face. If she did, she worried that it would destroy the good feelings she was experiencing. Instead she looked at the wall behind it and tried thinking of Calamaro.

Something about the stranger intrigued her and so she imagined him being her husband while her child, the starfish, was being nourished by her breast milk. Maybe when the baby got older, Calamaro would teach it to ride a horse and shoot a gun. Father and son would go hunting for coyote or pronghorn while mother stayed at home and did housework, eagerly waiting for her men to get back. It was all just so splendid. She couldn't stand it any longer.

June grabbed the starfish in her hands and hugged it tightly. She didn't feel sick anymore.

"Mother loves you."

# CHAPTER NINE

Calamaro was enjoying Stacklee's company. The man was kind without being feminine, tough without being an asshole.

"You headed somewhere in particular?" Stacklee said, downing another whiskey shot. "Or are you just drifting through this wonderful desert of ours?"

"I had to get as far away from home as possible," Calamaro said.

"Where's home?"

"New Jersey."

Stacklee said, "So it's bad back east? I always hear people talking about how great it is."

Calamaro put the shot glass to his lips but then put it down. "Not that great."

"I guess all sorts of shit happens everywhere. Can't escape it, eh?"

"Nope."

Stacklee could see that the topic of conversation had changed Calamaro's mood. He went from happily drunk to drunkenly sullen. "Sorry I brought it up."

"My fault," Calamaro said. "I guess I never expect for the past to come up in conversation even though it always does. One memory can crush my peace of mind in a second."

Stacklee screwed the top back on the whiskey. "Something happened to you, huh? Something bad?"

"Yeah," Calamaro said. The color drained from his face.

"I need to keep my big mouth shut."

"No, don't worry about it," Calamaro said. "I think about it anyway so there's no use in hiding it. I had a family once. Wife and daughter. They were killed."

Stacklee dropped his head and looked at the floor. "Sorry to hear that. I really am."

"I know things like that happen all the time but it wasn't from a sickness or accident. A bunch of Union soldiers killed them both. Thought my wife was a spy for the Confederates since she had family in Kentucky."

"Shit," Stacklee said. "I don't know what to say."

"You don't have to say anything but now you know why I'm exploring this wonderful desert." Calamaro forced a somber smile.

"I was you, I wouldn't tell Betty about it. That's the kind of thing makes her cry. She's tough and all but she's still a woman."

Calamaro nodded. "I think I'll head back to my room. Need to rest, get my head right."

"I understand. You take care," Stacklee said.

Calamaro left the brothel and walked back to the hotel. He had enjoyed spending time with Stacklee. Though he had never known a black man personally, Calamaro never had anything against Negroes. The ones he did come in contact with had been no different than the white people he knew. They might not have been as well-dressed or well-educated but they had the same virtues and vices as anyone else. For that reason, Calamaro never understood why people gave Negroes so much trouble.

Nix Morrow and his two friends were a different story. Calamaro had known people like that his whole life. They were bullies, plain and simple. It was satisfying to see them intimidated.

Then Calamaro thought about the gold.

There were rumors that a renegade Confederate soldier

named Bert Cavanaugh stole a cache of gold and hid it in Screwhorse. Cavanaugh disappeared and now the gold was up for grabs. Calamaro thought it might be nice to find that gold and move on to California where he could start a new life.

Once he was in his hotel room, Calamaro laid on the bed without even taking his boots off. He stared at the water stains on the ceiling. The stains were in the shape of a woman's shoe. Then there was the sound of high heels on a hardwood floor and soon, the smell of the worn leather of a woman's shoe mixed with perfume.

His eyes were focused on the stain until his eyelids fluttered and he fell into drunken sleep while being lulled by the clip-clopping of the heels. Memories bombarded him and he fell back into the dream full of naked, tattooed women and a bank vault full of corpses.

Calamaro awoke to the sound of someone screaming in the next room.

"What the hell?" he said, sliding off his bed. He stood by his door and listened.

The scream moved from the room next door into the hallway. A woman's voice screamed, "Bastard! Bastard! Bastard!"

There was another scream but this time it was a man shouting, "You nigger bitch! Get your ass back here!" Calamaro opened his door and peered out. He saw the woman and was confused. The woman was white.

The man walked into the hallway. He was a large man with a thick purple beard that ended in grotesque curls. He grabbed the woman by the throat. "Get back in there and take your lickings!" Again the woman fought but quickly gave in.

Calamaro stepped out into the hallway. He said, "Problem?"

Both the man and woman looked at him strangely. They both said, "What?"

Calamaro took a step closer. "Is there a problem here?

Looks like you're giving the woman some trouble."

The woman said, "Mind your business, will you?" She took the man by the arm and pulled him into her room. She shouted over her shoulder. "Cocksucker!"

As the door swung closed, Calamaro saw the man with the purple beard punch the woman in the side of the head. The door shut.

Calamaro put his hand on the knob and turned. It was locked. He knocked softly with his knuckles. "Hey," he said.

The woman inside shouted and then the door opened. Standing there naked and bruised, the woman said, "What the fuck do you want now, asshole?"

Calamaro said, "Move."

Behind her, the man with the purple beard grabbed a gun from his holster which was lying on a chair. As he brought it up, Calamaro pulled the woman into the hallway and pulled his own gun.

A bullet whizzed by Calamaro's head. He brought his weapon up. His pistol burped and sent a bullet into the room, hitting the man in the neck. The blast singed some curls of the purple beard.

From behind him, a fist hit Calamaro in the back. He shoved the woman back and said, "Go."

"Asshole! You killed him!" she screamed, running down the stairs and out of the hotel.

Calamaro stood there still a little bit confused but figured it was just another one of those things that happens when a man and woman get together. Private passions have a way of turning into crazy games. Why that woman let the man treat her like that, he'd never know.

The man was on the floor, the gurgling coming up from his throat sounding like farts at the bottom of a well. Calamaro walked in the room and looked down at the dying man.

"You had to pull your gun, huh?" Calamaro said.

There was no response, only more gurgling.

"You want a doctor?"

More gurgling.

The man's purple beard started to move. The hairs twirled around like dizzy insect legs.

Calamaro took a step back.

As the purple beard's movements got more violent, the dying man lifted his gun hand again and pointed it at Calamaro. Through thick phlegm and blood, he said, "Yig." He cocked the gun. "Yog." He pulled the trigger.

Calamaro was nearly hypnotized by the purple beard and felt the bullet graze the top of his head. There was no use in bringing the man to the doctor now. He went down to a crouch and sent two bullets into the man's chest.

The man was dead.

Standing up, Calamaro holstered his pistol and stared down at the corpse. There was no doubting it. The man with the purple beard was as dead as a doornail. But why the hell were the beard hairs still moving? It was a macabre sight that made Calamaro walk quickly out of the room.

# CHAPTER TEN

Before he went to the brothel, Bluford Barnes decided to walk around the town and take in the sights. He wanted to be careful to steer clear of that Hard Candy Kid fellow but other than that, it should prove to be valuable time spent checking out the possibilities.

As he walked past the barber shop, he heard voices behind him.

One of them said, "Hey Nix, look at that guy dressed up like an Englishman. Must be lost."

"Shut up, Ryan. We got work to do," said the other.

The voices trailed off in the other direction and for that Bluford was grateful. In every town he went to, there were always a few troublemakers who would stop at nothing to harass a stranger, especially one dressed as immaculately as he. Besides, he didn't consider himself a fighter of any sort and felt that there was no shame in running away from a confrontation if there was any chance of physical harm.

He stopped at the General Store and looked out on the horizon. The Indians were still there, their camps a little bit closer now. That disturbed Bluford but he planned to be out of town before anything happened.

Putting on a big smile, he walked into the General Store. He was greeted by a man with a bigger smile than his own.

"Hello there!" the man said.

"Good day, sir."

"What can I do you for?"

Bluford shrugged. "Well sir, I don't know if I even came in here for any one thing. I just came into town for a bit and thought I'd have a look around. You have a nice establishment here."

The man smiled. "Thank you. I appreciate that. My name is Tom Duma." He extended his hand and Bluford took it.

"Bluford Barnes."

"What line of business you in, Mr. Barnes?"

"Oh, a little of this and a little of that. Most recently I've been in the position of salesman."

Tom Duma's eyes lit up. "Got anything of interest with you?"

"Sorry, no. I don't have my supplies with me at the moment."

Tom said, "Aw, that's too bad. I'm always in the market for new wares. People in this town are always after something new. In fact, just last week a man from Rhode Island came through. You ever been to Rhode Island?"

"No, sir, I haven't. Heard it's nice, though."

"Yeah, well, this man came through and brought a few boxes of things he was selling. Things from Tibet, he said. That's somewhere in Asia, I believe," Tom said. He pointed behind him at a group of jars filled with dark green candy-sticks. "Brought some candy called Tcho-Tchos. I wasn't going to buy it at first being that I carry dozens of different types of candies from all over but some people in town had a taste of the Tcho-Tchos and insisted that I buy it for my store and so that's what I did."

"They taste good, those Tcho-Tchos?"

"Well, they're not to my liking. Personally I think the things taste a bit too much like sweet fish but I never was one for the sweets. Of course I don't know shit when it comes to that sort of thing. Hell, the Hard Candy Kid comes in nearly every day to buy one and that man knows his candy."

At the mention of the Hard Candy Kid, Bluford cleared his throat and said, "Well, I do regret that I don't have anything to sell you but I would like to purchase a few items."

"I can help you with that, for sure," Tom said. He tapped his fingertips on the counter. "But before I do, I have one question."

"Alright."

"Are you a drinking man, Mr. Barnes?"

"Uh, well, I have been known to get my tongue wet with some whiskey on occasion, yes."

Tom said, "I think I might have something you'd be interested in." He lowered his voice. "Ever hear of Ass Juice?"

# CHAPTER ELEVEN

June left the starfish and walked back to her room. As she sat on her bed, she wondered if she'd ever get married and have children. An image of her future popped into her head. She saw herself making dinner for a group of baby starfish who were seated around a table.

As she fantasized, her nausea subsided. June could feel her strength coming back. Her skin didn't feel so hot and clammy. It was time to get back to earning some money.

June freshened up, feeling more and more normal as she did so. In the back of her mind, she still thought about raising a family of baby starfish but now it was only a slight fantasy. When she was done getting ready, she walked downstairs and perused the room. There were a few strangers in the place and a few of them looked interesting. One in particular caught her eye. It was another handsome stranger, but not the one that Betty had been talking to.

This stranger was tall and swarthy. He looked like he was one of those Italians. The man looked strong, too, as if he could ravage her for hours without breaking a sweat. June thought how nice it would be to stick her four feet in his face, make him lick her dirty toes.

June wiggled her ass and made sure to keep the man in view. She hopped up onto the bar and sat there waiting for him to look over at her. When he did, June would use all her feminine charms to lure him over.

\* \* \*

When Bluford came back from the General Store, he decided to finally visit the brothel. He was sitting at the bar when he saw the guy in the donkey mask. The man had come in with two other men. One was old and bearded while the other was tall and olive-skinned. It was a strange but intriguing trio. Bluford knew something was going to happen. There was just something about those men. So when the swarthy man walked over to the bar, Bluford said, "Excuse me, sir. Buy you a drink?"

The man looked over but said nothing.

That did not deter Bluford. "I'm sorry for bothering you. Just passing through?"

"None of your goddamn business."

"The reason why I'm asking is because I can see you're a traveler like me and…"

"Shut up, will you?" The man was visibly agitated.

Bluford said, "Got it." He asked the bartender for a bottle of whiskey and then poured the man a drink. "Want that drink? Consider it payment for bothering you."

Some of the agitation left the man's face. He took the drink.

"My name is Bluford, by the way."

The man grunted. He took another drink and when he realized that Bluford was waiting for his name, he said, "Sergio."

"Pleasure to meet you, Sergio."

That was the extent of the conversation because then Sergio walked away and joined his friends.

Bluford was disappointed. He wanted to know more about the man because he and his partners looked like they had a purpose for being in town. Men who were planning on taking money from people always had the same look. There was an intensity there that many people weren't able to see but a professional confidence man could spot it pretty easily.

Bluford wanted to know exactly what they were planning.
And whether he could benefit from it.

* * *

Leonard was just about to take his first sip of whiskey when Clayton slapped him on the back.

"Hey old man, get a look at these girls! Really something, right? Makes my mouth water."

"Yeah, they're pretty."

"Just pretty? They're goddamn angels!" Clayton turned to Sergio. "What do you think? You like them?"

Sergio was holding a glass of whiskey up to his lips without taking a drink. He was taking in the sights slowly, taking time to look at each and every whore. If he was going to spend money to be with a girl, he didn't want his decision to be a rash one.

"Yeah, Clayton. They're angels," Sergio said. "They just won't stay that way after you get to them, huh?"

Clayton laughed. "You got that right!"

Finally Sergio took a sip and was reminded how much he loved whiskey. Back in Andersonville, they didn't give the men anything to drink but tainted water. Sergio had quite a few friends who died due to the torture and neglect at the hands of those Confederate bastards. He'd seen men used in experiments involving animals and strange machines that cut off their feet. It was a miracle that Sergio ever survived so he vowed to savor every drink of whiskey.

Leonard said, "You boys want to get your pricks wet, go ahead. I'm staying down here. Maybe join a poker game."

"I still don't get why you won't just pay for a screw. Not like you have much time left on this earth. You think they got pussy in Hell?" Clayton scratched his beard through his donkey mask and laughed.

"Oh, shut the hell up and go pick out a girl so you

53

can get it out of your system. We have to get to planning how we're going to persuade the mayor to part with his gold."

Clayton laughed. "Persuade? That's a good one." He looked around and saw the two ladies at the bar and thought they'd both be nice to take up to one of the rooms upstairs. He'd heard that the whores in town had specialties and he had a hankering to experience it in person.

He left the table and walked over to the women. They both turned his way and smiled though he had a suspicion that they were smiling sarcastically.

Clayton said, "Hello, ladies."

The blonde one said, "Can we help you?"

"Sure hope you can."

The brunette said, "You going to a costume party or something? What's with the mask?"

"Just something I like to wear. Found it in a prison camp next to a wooden donkey if you can believe it."

The two women laughed.

"Name's Clayton and you are?"

"I'm Goldie and this is Blanche. We're the Brady sisters," the brunette said.

"Sisters? You really sisters?"

The women laughed but didn't answer.

"So, I got money to spend," Clayton said. "You ladies want to welcome me to your town?"

Clayton followed the women to their room. He wasn't sure what he wanted. Whenever he was with a whore, he ended up asking for a hand job or a simple screw. But it seemed like a waste to ask for the same from these girls since Screwhorse whores were supposed to be so talented. "Hey ladies, let me ask you something. You two have a specialty?"

They laughed. Goldie said, "We sure do."

"And what would it be?"

In unison, the women burped loudly and smiled. "Let's see your pecker," Blanche said. Clayton sat down on the bed and pulled his dick out.

"Start yanking," Goldie said. As Clayton pleasured himself, the women instructed him while they leaned over and let out burp after burp into his face.

Blanche said, "You like that? Can you smell what we had for dinner?"

"We had four sausages," Goldie said. "Each!"

Even through the donkey mask, Clayton was overwhelmed by the warm stench of their belching. He used his hand on himself, stroking slowly at first and then picking up the pace when the burps became louder and more forceful.

After ten minutes, he was close to finishing. "I'm ready, ladies!"

Blanche put her mouth up to the nose holes of Clayton's mask while Goldie put her mouth to his ear.

As the ladies let out two thunderous burps, Clayton ejaculated onto the floor. Ecstasy rushed through his body as he deeply inhaled the smell of sausages.

"So, about payment," Goldie said. She wasn't wasting any time.

Clayton paid the women and stood up. "That sure was nice."

Blanche said, "Okay, honey, you go ahead downstairs and have yourself a drink. Come on back if you feel like having another go at the Brady sisters."

With a wide smile hidden by his donkey mask, Clayton buttoned his pants and left the room. The stories were true. Screwhorse really did have the best girls. When he got downstairs he saw Leonard talking to a whore who was on her knees examining his hands.

"You have such beautiful hands. Look at these fingers. Beautiful," the woman said.

Clayton leaned close to Leonard's ear. "What the hell's this?"

"This is Angie. She said she loves my hands," Leonard

said. He had told himself he wasn't going to get a girl but this Angie just came up to him, going on and on about how nice his hands were.

Angie said, "Your fingernails are beautiful, too. Hey. How about I take you upstairs?"

"I don't know. I think I'm just too damn old for what you're planning to do to me."

"Oh, you are not!" Angie smiled. She brought her hand up to Leonard's nose and caressed it. "You have a beautiful nose, too."

Clayton laughed. This Angie was one weird whore.

"Well," Leonard said. "Maybe you'd like my friend." He pointed to Sergio.

"Him? He looks scary, not nice like you. Are you sure you don't want me? I'll let you bind my feet."

"What?"

"I'll let you bind my feet. I learned it from a Chinaman used to come to town."

Leonard shrugged. "Not sure that's something I'd enjoy."

"Guess it's your loss, then," Angie said. She looked at Clayton. "How about you? Care to take off that donkey mask so I could take a look at your nose?"

"Sorry, sweetie, but no. The mask stays," Clayton said. "Besides, Those Brady sisters were quite enough."

Both rejections made Angie get up abruptly and stomp away.

Leonard cocked his head, turning his ear toward the door. "You hear that?"

Sergio nodded. "Yeah, those goddamn Indians are making more noise."

"They got some nerve doing that so close to town, eh?" Clayton said.

"Yeah and I don't like it. I'd like to get the job done before anything happens. I don't need to be trying to get out of town in the middle of a fucking Indian attack."

Clayton said, "Those redskins aren't going to do a goddamn thing. They just like dancing around fires, eating buffalo balls and shit."

"Even so, keep your eyes open," Sergio said. He drank one more shot of whiskey and then slammed his glass down. "Okay, I'm getting a girl now. Stay out of trouble, Clay, got it?"

"Yeah," Clayton said, adjusting his mask.

Sergio got up from the table and approached a whore who was sitting on the bar, dangling her feet. He had noticed her a while ago and could tell that she was looking at him. It was as if she had already picked him and not the other way around.

Then Sergio saw the extra foot that came out of each of her ankles. It would be the first time that he had a girl with four feet and he thought that might be just the thing to relax him before the job. He stood next to her and tried to smile as best he could. It came out like a frustrated frown.

He said, "You available?"

The older woman behind the bar answered for her. "No, she's not. She hasn't been feeling well."

The young whore said, "Oh, Betty, I'm feeling better now." She turned to Sergio and smiled. "What're you looking for? My feet can give you one hell of a jerk." She hopped off the bar. "My name's June."

Sergio said, "Let's go upstairs."

"You don't waste any time, do you?

"No," Sergio said. "I don't."

# CHAPTER TWELVE

Calamaro walked downstairs. Kersey was standing behind the front desk, shaking his head. "Those gunshots I heard?"

"Yeah," Calamaro said.

"What the fuck for?"

"It was unavoidable. A man upstairs was knocking around a lady. You probably saw her running out, didn't you? Well, her man didn't like me interfering and so he started something I had to finish."

Kersey sighed. "Yeah, should've known that Merrick bastard would go and do something like that. I don't know why I even let him stay here."

"I take it the sheriff will want to talk to me," Calamaro said.

"Yeah, probably but that'll cause me just as much trouble. I'll see what I can do about sorting it all out."

"Much obliged."

"Just make sure you don't make any more enemies in here, okay?"

"I'll do my best," Calamaro said. He took a step towards the door but then turned around. He said, "There a good place to eat around here?"

"If you want a hot meal, your best bet is Tom Duma's place. He owns the General Store but Mrs. Duma also cooks meals there, too. Of course you could also try the brothel but the food isn't too much to my liking. I figure that's on account

of the fact that people go there for the women not the grub."

"I guess I'll try the General Store. A hot meal would be good." Calamaro walked out of the hotel. He walked down the street and saw a short, bald man punching a horse.

As Calamaro passed, the man said, "Hey you."

Calamaro stopped. "Yeah?"

"You got candy?"

"I look like a child to you?" Calamaro laughed.

The man's eyes glazed over. "You're a funny guy, huh?"

"If you think so," Calamaro said. He looked into the man's eyes and for the first time in his life, he got goose bumps. The man's eyes were milky and cold. They belonged in a dead man's skull. Calamaro didn't want to spend anymore time looking into them so he nodded and walked away.

From behind him, the man's voice said, "If I see you again, you better have some candy. Some *hard* candy."

# CHAPTER THIRTEEN

Nix knocked on William Lyons' door. He didn't like disturbing the man at his house but he was just too damned angry at that stranger to wait. Chaps and Ryan stood behind him.

There were sounds of children playing and then heavy footsteps. The door opened.

"What is it?" Lyons stood in the doorway. He was tall, blond, and good-looking, just the type of man one would expect to be running for political office. William Lyons was well-known for both his charisma as well as his devotion to his family and to the church. He was also known for his killing.

Nix said, "Need to talk to you. This a bad time?" He saw Lyons' two sons running around a table, smiling and yelling up a storm.

"I'm with my family right now, you can see that. What the hell's so important you can't wait till tomorrow?"

"I, uh, just need to talk to you about a little situation we have. With a stranger. Some guy came into town and started some trouble."

Lyons said, "That black eye of yours, that the trouble you're talking about?"

"Yeah."

Lyons lowered his voice. "Some cocksucker gives you a black eye and you come interrupt me spending time with my family? What do you reckon I do, go get a search party and lynch the cocksucker?"

Nix blushed. His face now almost matched his eye. "There's more than that, Mr. Lyons. The guy punched me when I wasn't even looking. That's a plain old coward if you ask me, know what I'm saying?"

Lyons poked his head out of the door and looked at Chaps and Ryan. "Well, where the hell were these guys at? Why didn't they do something? You telling me the three of you couldn't handle one fucking guy?"

Nix said, "Uh, it's not like that…"

From behind Lyons, children's voices said, "Daddy! Daddy!"

"Nix, I'm going to go back in the house and play with my boys."

"What are we going to do about it?"

"We're not going to do anything. You want to take care of it, do it."

Lyons slammed the door closed. Nix frowned and then turned back to walk down the stairs. Chaps and Ryan followed.

The front door opened again and Lyons stuck his head out.

"Fine, Nix. I'll look into it. Just keep your ass out of trouble until I get back to you, you hear?"

"Sure thing, Mr. Lyons. Thank you."

The door slammed again.

# CHAPTER FOURTEEN

Rebecca Bywater was still looking out the window when she heard a woman's voice from the room next door. "Give me that snake, you bastard! Give it to me! Let it spit! I want it comin' outta my ears!"

She had never heard firsthand the sound of a woman actually enjoying sex. It was going to be something she had to get used to.

Rebecca fixed her hair, changed her clothes, and then walked downstairs.

Betty was behind the bar, talking to a large man who was smoking a red cigarette. When she saw Rebecca, Betty said, "Hey honey, I want you to meet someone."

"Oh?" Rebecca said.

"Yeah, this here's Black Boned Keith. He's just been asking me if I got any new girls. I told him that maybe I did."

Rebecca made sure she put on a sweet face. The way Betty was talking, it sounded like she was leaning toward hiring her on. That was a good sign. "Well, it's nice to meet you."

"Pleasure to meet you, honey," Keith said. "I hope you don't mind saying but you're a pretty one. So, you work here now?"

Rebecca took his hand and shook it delicately. "I don't know." She looked at Betty. "Do I?"

"Yeah, I guess you do," Betty said.

Black Boned Keith slapped his leg. "Well, isn't that just

great! I come into town expecting the same old entertainment and I get a fresh one right off the stagecoach."

Betty smiled. "Slow down, Keith. I ain't sure she's ready for you just yet. How about you let the girl mingle and then if she doesn't find a better prospect, we'll see if she'll settle for you."

Keith laughed. "You let this girl know what fun she'll have, I bet she'll settle for me right now."

"Didn't you already have Angie? What? She didn't satisfy you?"

"Of course she did but you know I've been away from home so long. I got some making up to do."

"Well, let Rebecca mingle and maybe she'll come back." Betty laughed and put her hand on Rebecca's shoulder. "Go ahead, sweetie."

Rebecca smiled and looked at Betty who nodded her head in the direction of the tables full of drunken men. It was up to her, the new whore, to impress her boss by getting the attention of all those potential customers. So she did just that, walking by the tables, brushing past some men with her hips while running her fingers through the dirty hair of others.

There was one man in particular she thought was interesting. He looked wealthier than the others and a little bit older. Rebecca decided that he was her mark.

She put her mouth close to his ear and whispered. "You want to take a break from your poker game?"

The man looked up at her and squinted. "Who are you?"

"My name's Rebecca and it's nice to meet you, Mr....?"

"Not in the mood for pussy. Go sell yours somewhere else."

Rebecca's mouth fell open. Her first instinct was to slap the man across the mouth and cuss at the son of a bitch. But that wouldn't do any good. Not with Betty watching. Instead, she smiled slyly, winked at another man, and moved on to another table. That's when Betty called her over to the bar. When she got there, Black Boned Keith was shaking his head.

He said, "Of all the men you decide to come on to, you had to pick that cranky bastard."

"How's I to know what a son of a bitch he is?"

Betty said, "You weren't. But you did good. You went on like it didn't bother you. Truth is old Frank Dozier over there doesn't come in for the girls, he comes in to play cards. He always loses, too, but that doesn't matter. His daddy was rich and left him everything when he died."

Keith said, "You want to know how his daddy died?"

Betty threw her hands up. "Oh my god, not this story again!"

"Let me tell her. She don't know it." He laughed as Betty walked away. "You see, honey, Adam Dozier, that's Frank Dozier's rich daddy, owned a bunch of mines all around Screwhorse. Mined for silver mostly but occasionally he'd find other things worth selling. One day he was supervising one of the mines and there they are, digging and digging, doing whatever miners do and guess what they find all buried fifty feet under the ground?"

"What?" Rebecca wasn't that interested but knew that Black Boned Keith seemed to be a regular customer and therefore that meant he liked to spend money. It was in her best interest to stay on his good side.

"They found teeth." Keith paused for dramatic effect. "And I don't mean animal teeth. I mean human teeth, thousands and thousands of human teeth. One of the miners actually ran out screaming, ran away and never came back. Adam Dozier had no use for nonsense like that so he went in to see for himself and guess what happened?"

"I don't know. What?"

"According to all his men, Adam Dozier let out a scream like all bloody hell and then tried to turn tail and run away but tripped and fell right in a pile of teeth. The men were too scared or confused to do anything because Dozier was both screaming and laughing until he sunk down into the teeth and they were only able to see his fingers. Then soon he stopped making noise." He paused, widening his eyes. "He drowned."

Rebecca smiled. She was expecting Keith to start laughing, telling her that it was just a joke and that the real Adam Dozier had died of old age. Instead, he just looked at her with a serious expression and nodded.

He said, "You understand? He didn't drown in water. He drowned in teeth."

She didn't know what he expected her to say so she just said, "Well."

"I know it's strange but strange things do happen."

"Thanks for the story," Rebecca said. "I guess that explains why Frank over there is such a cranky son of a bitch." She touched his arm lightly. "Keith, where's the General Store at? I need to pick up a few things."

"Just go out the door and turn right. Down the ways a bit. Place is owned by Tom Duma and his wife. Good people."

"Thank you," she said. As she was walking out, she caught a glimpse of a man staring at her. He was dressed nicely, even too nicely considering he was drinking whiskey in a whorehouse. Wasn't he on the stagecoach with her?

Normally she didn't like people staring at her but now that she was a working woman, she knew she'd have to get used to it if she wanted to make money. So Rebecca smiled at the man but continued to walk out. Maybe she would approach him when she came back.

Once she was outside, Rebecca stood out on the porch for a few minutes, taking in the sights and sounds of Screwhorse. Main Street was bustling with men, women, and horses. Again, she felt that dread in her gut. Rebecca hoped it was just nerves.

She walked down towards the General Store and went

inside. A smiling man behind the counter greeted her.

"Hello there! What could I do for you?"

Rebecca gave the man a great big smile. "I just moved in town so I need a few things."

The man put out his hand and Rebecca shook it. "My name's Tom Duma."

"Rebecca Bywater."

"You staying at the hotel?"

"No, I'm staying at Betty's."

Tom Duma's smile faded. "Oh."

"What's wrong? I thought this town was okay with….. you know, women working there."

"It is. The town never had a problem with it. It's just that..."

"Let me guess. You're a religious man?" Rebecca said. She always found it absurd how many of the men who object to brothels on religious grounds are the men who secretly harbor passions that are even filthier than anything you'd find in a whorehouse.

Tom Duma said, "No, no. It's just that whenever I see such a young, pretty woman I tend to get a little sad thinking of her selling herself to all those dirty men. I'm not judging you, please don't think that. Things go on there that can hurt a lady. It's just discouraging. All those filthy men."

Rebecca patted his hand. "Oh, rest assured I'll make the men take a bath before they have a go at me." She smiled.

"You're a funny one, Miss Bywater," Tom said. A smile was back on his face as he continued to help Rebecca with her order. When they were done, he slipped something into her hand.

"What's this?"

"Just some medicine," he said. "For women. You feel itchy or have any sores...down there, you just rub some of that on. My wife just ordered it all the way from Thompson, New Jersey. She wants me to give it to any of the girls who come in here."

Rebecca said, "Uh, okay, well I don't know if I'll need it but thank you. I guess."

As she opened the door to leave, a man walked through the doorway and bumped into her.

"Excuse me, miss," the man said. "That was clumsy of me."

"Oh, don't you worry about it. It was my fault," Rebecca said. "I'm Rebecca Bywater."

"I'm Calamaro," the man said, taking his hat off.

Rebecca practically swooned as she looked into Calamaro's eyes and hoped that he would visit the brothel and become one of her very first customers. "Well, I must be going. It was very nice meeting you, Calamaro."

"It was my pleasure, Miss Bywater," Calamaro said. He pushed the door open for her.

She left the store and walked quickly back to Betty's. The run-in with Calamaro made her eager to get to work. Her womanhood was warm and aching for a man. Now all she had to do was find one that'd be a suitable substitute for Calamaro.

* * *

Tom Duma smiled at Calmaro and said, "Good evening, sir! How can I be of service?"

"I was told your wife is the one to see for some good food."

"Oh that she is. I'll go get her to make you a plate. Should be no more than ten, fifteen minutes."

"Thank you. Tell her she could take her time. I got nowhere to be," Calamaro said. He stood against the counter behind which was a wide array of medicines, candies, cooking supplies, and bottles full of unidentifiable liquid. He watched Tom Duma walk into the backroom. Then there were voices. The husband softly asked his wife if she could prepare a plate for the stranger. The wife's sultry but annoyed voice chattered away. She was just about to go upstairs and clean up. She didn't feel like making any more food. There was another minute of arguing until the wife finally relented. She'd make a small plate of scraps.

Tom Duma walked out of the backroom with a smile plastered to his face. "Sorry about that, sir. My wife isn't feeling well but she'll make you a plate."

"Please thank her for me."

"I will, I will." Tom put his palms down on the counter. "Is there anything else I can get you while you wait? We got the best selection of hard candies, Mexican cigars, and even…" He stopped and looked towards the door to the backroom.

"And even what?"

Tom Duma whispered. "Ever hear of Ass Juice?"

Calamaro shook his head.

"It's made in the south, hit its peak back before the war. During all the fighting, they didn't make much of it, though. It's still hard to come by. You see, it's made like regular whiskey but once it's done, they get a whole bunch of dirty, sweaty whores and make them bathe in it. You know, clean up all their girly parts with the whiskey. They sit in it about a week and don't come out of there for even a minute."

"Sounds pleasant," Calamaro said.

"Well, personally I don't touch the stuff. I got a bad stomach. But all the men in town swear by it." He looked to the backroom again. "The wife doesn't like me selling it so I have to sneak it. Got a couple bottles left, if you're interested. Earlier today I actually just sold a bottle to another man from out of town. Is he a friend of yours? Did you come into town together?"

"No, I came alone," Calamaro said. "I'm guessing the price is a bit higher than regular whiskey."

"A little bit, yes, but Ass Juice is worth it, I'm telling you. I swear you can taste cunny and girl-ass in every sip." Tom Duma smiled. "Or so I've heard."

"Maybe another time."

"I even have a bottle that's just full of feet. I mean, they had a bunch of whores just soak their feet in it."

"No thanks."

"Suit yourself, stranger."

Mrs. Duma walked out of the backroom with a plate in her hands. She scowled at the two men and said, "Food's done."

"Thank you, ma'am," Calamaro said. The plate was practically slammed down in front of him. He dug into the lukewarm meat and corn.

Tom Duma nodded to his wife and swatted her on the arm. "Make us some coffee, will you?"

"Oh, of course. Not like I have anything better to do." She walked out of the room in a huff.

"Nice lady," Calamaro said. He smirked. Women like that always confused him. They acted tough but always seemed to want men to treat them like fragile flowers. They should make up their minds.

"She gets like that sometimes. She can be as sweet as candy, though, hugging and kissing me all over but then all of a sudden she turns into a mean old thing. Good times do make up for the bad ones, though."

Calamaro thought about what Mrs. Duma would be like in bed. Did she dominate her husband there, too?

Soon the plate was empty and Calamaro wiped his mouth on his sleeve. He thanked Tom again.

"You're very welcome." Tom moved his head in close. "Don't mind me asking but what happened to your ear?"

Calamaro licked his fingers clean. "A kid shot me."

"A kid shot you?"

"Yep."

"He have reason to?"

Calamaro said, "None that I saw."

"So it was just some kid took a gun and shot you?"

"Called himself the Clementine Kid if that holds any meaning to you. Wanted to rob me so he took a shot. I shot back. Kid's dead but my bullet ain't what did it."

"Then what did?"

"Indians."

Tom frowned. "Oh."

"Don't feel so bad though. I don't think he was so innocent. Kid looked like he'd served in the war. Probably done more killing than you and I could imagine."

"War will do strange things to a man," Tom said. "Hell, there's a fellow in town who fought and came back all nervous and always shaking. He took to hiring whores to tie him to a bed and put scorpions all over his body while he's lying there naked."

Calamaro squinted. "Naked?"

"Yes sir. I'm pretty sure he wasn't like that before the war. That's what I heard. Maybe I'm wrong and maybe he was always a bit crazy."

"I've noticed that every man has some sort of dirty desire they like to keep hidden," Calamaro said.

Tom laughed. "Still, it's damn queer. I'm glad I didn't get wrapped up in the fighting. The hell if I was going to risk my ass for something like that."

"Sometimes a man don't got a choice. Everyone around you doing something, you might do it just so you don't stick out and look peculiar even if that means doing something you'd rather not do."

Tom opened his mouth to respond but a noise from the backroom interrupted him. It was a low grunt and then a sound like something heavy hitting the floor.

"Christ!" Tom ran to the backroom. Calamaro dug into his pockets, pulled out an amount of money he thought the food was worth, and then walked out.

He wondered why the sheriff hadn't talked to him yet. Usually when he came through a town, the law met up with him within minutes. They always gave him the same speech about how their town is different from the others and how it would not tolerate trouble of any kind, big or small. Calamaro noticed that the longer the speech, the more corrupt the town. Because the sheriff of Screwhorse did not come out to meet him, Calamaro was more than a little confused. He would have to be prepared for anything.

# CHAPTER FIFTEEN

Stacklee leaned in close to Betty's ear. "Something about those guys bother you, too?"

"I don't know. The guy in the mask is weird, I guess. And I hope June is going to be okay with that other one. He scares me." She looked over at the new customers. Stacklee usually had a knack for judging people so she tried to see what he was seeing.

Stacklee said, "The guy who went up with June. He doesn't seem like he's here to enjoy himself. Looks like he's just killing time."

"Most of the men come in here are killing time. You think there's something different about him?"

"He looked like he's waiting for something to happen or waiting to do something. I just don't like it."

"Keep an eye on him," Betty said. "What I'm really getting worried about is all that noise from the Indians. Getting worse and worse. I think I saw one of them last night walking around by the church."

"I imagine the sheriff's taking care of it best he could."

Betty laughed. "You think Doyle's going to do anything? Shit."

Their conversation was interrupted by the rising din of the Indians outside of town. After a few minutes it tapered off but it left the inhabitants of the brothel unsettled. It wasn't just drumming this time. There was also a deep voice that sang loudly, echoing through the town like an anxious church bell.

Stacklee said, "Hey, you want me to check on Mary? Make sure everything's okay?"

"Yeah, but try to do it without upsetting Timothy."

"Don't you worry, Betty," he said. "I'll treat him like a sweet little baby."

\* \* \*

Mary felt disgusted with herself.

The whole ordeal had been a messy and degrading lesson in what a woman has to do in order to please a man with connections to those in power. Hopefully Timothy would give his uncle, Mayor Douglas, a good report on what the brothel was doing. Maybe he'd even give her a compliment or two. Didn't the mayor hire girls for private parties that he threw for fellow politicians? Maybe Timothy would recommend Mary for that. There was sure to be a lot of money in it.

But the disgust was definitely an overwhelming factor as she sat on the bed covered in slime and semen. Timothy was lying on the bed next to her, snoring loudly. What she wanted to do the most was wake him up and get him out of there but since he had paid to stay overnight, there was nothing she could do but wait there just in case he woke up and wanted another screw.

There was a knock at the door.

"Mary? It's Stacklee. You two okay in there?"

She rushed to the door. "Shhh! He's sleeping," Mary said, stepping into the hallway.

"Lord, look at you. You're a mess," Stacklee said. "What's that smell?"

"You really don't want to know the answer to that."

"Well, I just wanted to make sure that boy wasn't giving you any trouble."

"No. I'm fine."

Stacklee patted her shoulder. "You need anything?"

"Maybe just a drink. You mind bringing a bottle up here when you get a chance?"

"Sure thing, Mary. You hang in there," Stacklee said.

As she watched him walk away, Mary thought Stacklee would make a good lover though she knew that would be completely inappropriate. Mary would just have to make due with thinking about it.

She walked back into her room and saw that Timothy was sitting up in bed. He was holding a tentacle over his mouth. "Look, I just grew a mustache!"

Mary chuckled nervously and walked back to bed. It was going to be a long day.

# CHAPTER SIXTEEN

In the hotel, Nix pulled Kersey into a backroom and pushed him up against the wall. "The stranger that came into town, he have a room here?"

"Which one? There were a few strangers," Kersey said.

"The one with the busted up ear."

Kersey said, "Yeah." He wasn't afraid of Nix. The guy was an overgrown bully who loved throwing his muscle around. The only thing remotely scary about him was the fact that he worked for William Lyons.

"We're going to wait here and when he comes in, you're going tell us, know what I'm saying?"

"Yes."

Nix let go of him and walked out of the room. Ryan giggled and Chaps wore a giant smile.

Chaps said, "I thought you said William told you to wait for him."

"We're just going to fool with him a bit," Nix said. He saw Chaps taking out a cigarette. "Put that shit away. You know I can't stand the smell."

Chaps smiled wider, kept the cigarette in his mouth for a few seconds, and then took it out. "Sorry."

They walked outside and leaned up against the building. A herd of cattle silently grazed nearby. Ryan said, "You think those are Black Boned Keith's animals?"

"Must be. Herds don't usually come through

Screwhorse," Nix said.

"Something's wrong with them cows, you ever notice that?"

Chaps smiled wildly. "They look fine to me. Fine enough to eat, I'd say. I haven't had meat in a while."

Nix shrugged. "So we'll get a steak later."

Chaps walked away towards the herd. "I don't want steak."

"What the hell you doing?" Ryan said, watching Chaps as he walked up to the nearest cow, got down on his knees and slid underneath.

Nix squinted. "Shit. What in God's name?"

There he was, a skinny little man lying underneath a huge cow, chomping on the beast's belly. He took mouthful after mouthful of raw beef, tentacles, and milk-filled udders while he giggled. The animal he chewed on did nothing but make low groaning sounds. It didn't seem too bothered.

While chowing down, Chaps was back to thinking about his French horn. As he took a particularly thin tentacle into his mouth, he imagined it was the mouthpiece of his horn. He blew into it but there was no sound. Goddamnit, he thought, why did I have to lose that horn?

Chaps sucked on another tentacle. He hoped Nix was watching and that he was impressed with his sucking skills. Ever since he started working with the guy, he had been attracted to his bravado as well as his muscles. Though Chaps would never consider himself one of those strange men who liked to poke other men in the ass, he could not resist that primal attraction to Nix and he found himself wanting to do just about anything to earn the man's affection and approval.

Ryan said, "Chaps, get your skinny ass over here!" He was getting nauseous watching. There was white, green, and black goop all over Chaps' face.

Nix put his hands on his hips. "Jesus Christ, this is just disgusting."

Chaps stopped. He stood up, let out a thunderous burp, and walked back to Nix and Ryan.

Nix punched him in chest. "What in the hell was that?"

"Just wanted to try something new is all," Chaps said. He smiled and rubbed the spot that had been punched. "We all got to try something new sometime or else life gets a little boring."

Nix said, "If you weren't so good with a whip, I'd kick your ass. Now let's go back inside. I have an idea."

\* \* \*

Calamaro reached the hotel. Before he walked in, he lit a cigarette. As he looked through the window of the hotel, he noticed that Kersey was staring at him. The man looked nervous.

Letting the cigarette hang out of his mouth, Calamaro widened his eyes at Kersey who then nodded his head slightly. It was a nearly undetectable signal but a signal nonetheless. Calamaro walked down the alley next to the hotel and around the back to his wooden donkey.

He put his hand on it and said, "How you holding up, Sartana?"

With a slight push of a button, a small compartment opened up in the donkey's back leg. Calamaro took something out and slipped it into his jacket pocket. Then he pushed the compartment back, listening for the click to make sure it was locked, and walked into the back door of the hotel.

Kersey was standing in the hallway, worry still apparent on his wrinkled face. He gave a tiny gesture towards the stairs. Calamaro nodded and proceeded to go in that direction, the cigarette still hanging out of his mouth. He slowly opened the door to his room.

He said, "Should have told me you were dropping by, I'd have brought whiskey."

Nix was lying on the bed while Chaps stood on the

right side of it. From behind the door, Ryan jumped out and took Calamaro's gun from its holster. He threw the pistol onto the bed next to Nix.

"Well, you wouldn't have time to drink it, know what I'm saying?" Nix said, sitting up on the bed. His shirt sleeves were rolled up to reveal his bulging muscles.

"Not sure I do. I thought we settled this already. A guy can get the wrong idea if three men show up in his bedroom. You boys want me to take my pants off?" Calamaro smirked.

Ryan laughed but stopped when Nix looked his way.

"Look, asshole, I'm going to let one of my boys here have at you for a while. Teach you a lesson. Then I'm going to do what I do best." Nix tapped Ryan and pointed at Calamaro. "Go get him."

Ryan rushed forward like an angry child would. Calamaro could see that the guy had no real fighting experience. It took only one uppercut to send Ryan to the floor. He didn't stay down but instead grabbed for Calamaro's feet and was met with a kick to the jaw.

Calamaro pulled him by the shirt and stood him up on wobbly legs. "He had at me. Now what?"

Nix shook his head. "Lucky shot, motherfucker."

"Even so. He's finished. Are you?"

"Not by a mile," Nix said, reaching for his gun. Calamaro pulled Ryan close to him while reaching into his pocket, pulling out a half stick of dynamite. He bent down and stuck it into Ryan's left boot.

"Fuck you doing?" Ryan said. He pounded his fists on Calamaro's back. Nix had his gun pulled and was aiming it at Ryan's back. Chaps had his whip out but he just held it there like a limp dick.

Nix said, "Let him go, you sonovabitch."

"Anything you say," Calamaro said. He sent a fist into Ryan's gut that made him double over. Then he took the cigarette out of his mouth, lit the fuse on the dynamite and pushed

Ryan all the way to the window. Nix rolled off the bed and was trying to aim his gun but stopped as he watched Calamaro push Ryan forward. Glass shattered and the man went flying.

Nix's mouth opened in shock. He stood up and looked out the window. Ryan was lying on the ground below. Then there was an explosion. Ryan's legs disappeared in a mess of smoke, flesh, and bone.

From behind him Calamaro said, "Reach for the ceiling." Nix felt the barrel of a gun in his back. He turned his head to look at Chaps and saw that he was on the floor, bloody.

"Okay, asshole, you win. We're going." He turned slowly towards the door.

"That's right. You're going," Calamaro said. "But not through the door."

"What? You must be fucking kidding me."

Calamaro pushed the gun into his back hard. "That's right. Jump. I'll send your other boy after you."

"There's no way in hell." Nix was getting cocky but it ended as soon as the pistol slammed into the back of his head. "Okay, okay."

"Go ahead. Fly like an angel. You can try to land on your friend down there, maybe cushion your fall."

Nix climbed halfway out the window and saw Ryan moving. The stumps that had been his legs were smoking but he was definitely still alive and conscious. In fact, he was screaming for his mother. Nix yelled down at him. "Watch out!"

He jumped out of the window and landed right next to Ryan. Nix felt a bone break but wasn't sure if it was his arm or leg. Then he felt the pain in his knee. From above he heard a yelp and as soon as he looked up, Chaps landed on him ass first.

Calamaro stuck his head out of the window, the cigarette back in his mouth.

All three men on the ground looked up at him as he spoke.

"Feel free to drop by anytime, boys. I'll be waiting."

# CHAPTER SEVENTEEN

Sheriff Doyle heard the door open but did not look up from his newspaper. It was probably just another person complaining about the Hard Candy Kid. There was nothing anyone was going to do about it because the Kid was the meanest son of a bitch in the territory.

"Help you?" the sheriff said, still reading.

"Yes. You can start by putting down that fucking newspaper."

Sheriff Doyle's eyes widened as he put the newspaper down and turned in his chair. It was William Lyons.

"Sorry, didn't know it was you," Doyle said.

"So what? What if I was some nigger or Mexican coming in to kill you, what then? You just go on reading your newspaper while you get your throat cut by some dirty cocksucker?"

Doyle nodded his head. "You're right, you're right. I'm just tired is all."

"Well I'm tired and pissed off. Was spending time with my boys when Nix came by and told me there was some sort of stranger in town making trouble. I don't like taking time away from my family to deal with this shit."

"So why didn't you tell Nix to deal with it himself? He's good with a gun, ain't he?"

"Sometimes it's easier to just treat Nix and his boys like little babies. If I let them handle it, they're bound to fuck it up and give me a bigger headache."

Doyle pulled out a cigar and offered it to Lyons who shook his head, waving his hand away. "You know I don't smoke."

"I forgot," Doyle said. "I still don't know why you keep those boys around anyway."

"I have my reasons."

"So what'd you want me to do? I can't just go arrest him. You know we've been having some government assholes sticking their noses in my business, checking out how the town is run and how the jail is run, all that shit."

"You don't have to arrest him, just warn him. Last time I checked you were the law, right?"

Doyle stood up. "I'll take care of it, don't you worry."

"I'm not the one who should be worried."

The sheriff laughed, thinking that Lyons was referring to the stranger. Then the laughter faded when he realized that Lyons had meant to threaten him. "I'll take care of it."

"Okay then," Lyons said as he walked out.

Sheriff Doyle picked up the newspaper, threw it back down, and cursed. That William Lyons was really something. The man walked in as if he was the sheriff. Doyle figured there was no use fighting it, though. Lyons was the mayor's favorite citizen and so everything he did was okay.

Goddamnit, thought Doyle. He hated when Lyons barked orders at him. He had hope, though, that maybe someday Lyons would fall down, crack his head open, spill those crazy brains of his all over. He'd love to be there when it happened. That'd be nice.

The sheriff stood up, stretched, and walked outside so he could start looking for the stranger. He figured he would probably be in Betty's place since that's where most of the strangers ended up. Betty sure did have a good selection of whores. Doyle wasn't a customer, though. After all, he was the sheriff and he had an image to uphold. Occasionally he would meet up with one of the girls after hours and coerce her into giving him a free one. He especially liked that four-footed girl, June. Shit, she was a wild one with those twenty toes wiggling in his face while he screwed her. He often sucked the dirt out from underneath her toenails. For the rest of the night he'd feel that grit in his teeth and he loved it. She was a nice girl, too. Very polite and respectful.

Doyle walked over to Betty Black's place. Stacklee greeted him with a nod.

The sheriff grunted. "There a stranger in here, Stack?"

The black man said, "Yes sir, lot of 'em. One even came in wearing a donkey mask. Here's over there. You believe it?"

Sheriff Doyle looked over at the table and squinted in disgust when he saw the man in the donkey mask playing cards. "What the fuck, Stacklee? You throwing a party or something? Is he the one who caused trouble?"

Stacklee shook his head. "No, sir."

"Then who did?"

"Those boys work for Lyons caused most of it."

"I'm not asking you to be a goddamn judge, I want to know where the stranger is who came in here and caused trouble."

"Well, he's not here now if that's what you want to know." Stacklee shrugged and tried his hardest not to smile. "Must be he left town on account he knew you'd be looking for him. Probably real scared, pissed himself. You might be able to follow the trail."

"Don't get smart with me, boy. You play games with me, you'll get what's coming to you."

"Well, sir, like I said, I don't know nothing about where the stranger gone to. I'm just here to greet the customers."

Doyle squinted. "You like pretending you're just an ignorant Negro, that it?"

"No sir, not pretending. I am a Negro, sheriff. I saw it for myself when I looked in the mirror this morning."

The sheriff grunted and cursed. "Go get me a drink, will you?"

Stacklee walked over to the bar and tapped on it. "Betty, can you get the sheriff here a drink? His mouth must be dry, he's talking so much."

Betty held in a laugh and poured a shot of whiskey. Sheriff Doyle made a sour face and walked over to get it. He said, "Goddamn, Betty, you better tell your boy here that if he keeps running his mouth, I'll run him out of town before he can say Abraham Lincoln."

"Oh, Sheriff, he can't help it. He's just trying to be amusing," Betty said.

"Well, I'm not amused."

Behind the sheriff, Stacklee stood smirking. He resisted the urge to take the whiskey bottle and whack the sheriff upside the head with it. What held him back was his knowing that the threat to run him out of town was an empty one. Doyle had been saying that ever since Stacklee came to work in Screwhorse three years ago. He thought maybe the sheriff had a soft spot for Negros but was afraid to show it on account William Lyons and the mayor might not approve. Still, it would be sweet to just take the whiskey bottle and give him one good whack.

Doyle said, "Betty, your tits are hanging out, you know that?"

"Sure do, sheriff. You plan to arrest me for it?"

"I'd love to," he said, smiling. His mustache drooped down over his upper lip, just barely covering his crooked teeth. He finished his drink. "What I'm really here for is the stranger who started some ruckus here with some of the boys who work for Lyons. You see what happened?"

Betty said, "I heard you the first time and Stacklee told it like it is. Nix and them boys started in with Stacklee and the other man just came to his aid."

"Things get rough?"

Betty shrugged and when she did her breasts bounced, causing Doyle to stare wide-eyed at them. "Guess so."

"And you didn't think to come get me?"

"If I called you every time a fight broke out, you'd have to set up camp here."

Doyle's eyes were still on the breasts. "I don't mind some of the local boys roughhousing every once in a while if they got a few drinks in them but we're talking about a stranger we know nothing about. What if he's a wanted man or a crazy killer or something? You want someone shot dead right in the middle of your place?"

"I could just tell that wasn't going to happen."

"Well, I'd like to talk to this man anyway. He still here?"

"No. He left."

"And let me guess. You don't know where?"

Betty said, "No, I do not, sheriff but this town isn't that big so I'm guessing you're smart enough to find him."

Doyle finally took his eyes off Betty's mounds and said, "Guess I'll go find him then." He walked towards the door, passing Stacklee.

"Sheriff, I wish you the best of luck."

"Fuck you, Stack," Doyle said, walking outside and wishing that he had buried his face in Betty's tits.

# CHAPTER EIGHTEEN

Bluford thought stealing money from poker players was pretty easy. He had the brains and the tools to take a lot of money. He didn't necessarily consider it cheating. It was more like using all the advantages at hand in order to separate a fool and his money or in Bluford's case, separating many fools with lots of their money.

That's what he was planning to do when he went over to the brothel. He saw plenty of prospective suckers but settled on a table with a particularly easy mark. When Bluford introduced himself, the man just grunted and said, "I'm Frank. Sit down and shut up if you want to play."

So that's what they did. They played along with three other men who were the typical breed of poker players one would find in a small town.

Bluford was up quite a bit of money when he felt a tap on his shoulder. It was the black man who had been watching the door. He said, "Sir, there's someone who wants to see you."

"Can it wait? My friends and I are in the middle of a game," Bluford said. He thought adding that bit about his friends was a nice touch. It would put the other men at ease.

"No sir, it's urgent."

Bluford put his cards down on the table. "Sorry, boys, but I guess I'm folding this hand." He took the money he had won so far, got up, and followed the black man to the corner of the bar. Then he said, "So, who is it that wants to see me?"

The man said, "I do."

"Hey, what is this?" Bluford got nervous. He took a step back.

"Don't you worry. I ain't going to hurt you. I work here. Name's Stacklee. I just wanted to give you a little warning is all. I see you over there playing cards. You play a slick game."

"Yeah? I've always been pretty lucky. Nice of you to notice."

"Lucky? Shit. Too lucky. Personally, I don't care if you take money from assholes like Frank over there but if people start catching on, you can have a problem on your hands and that means I'll have to break it up. Betty doesn't need that kind of trouble."

Bluford smiled. "Are you kicking me out?"

"If I wanted to kick you out, I would've done it. In fact, the sheriff was just here and I could've just told him I had a cheater in the place," Stacklee said. "But the way I see it, a man's entitled to one warning before he gets his ass kicked out."

Bluford was starting to like the guy. He was straight-forward and honest even to a cheater. He was smart, too. Not many people could spot Bluford's tricks.

"I do appreciate it, Mr. Stacklee. Let me ask you, though. Was it that obvious?"

"Probably not to anyone else but I know a thing or two about card sharps. I grew up around them."

"As did I. Guess we have something in common."

Stacklee nodded. "Yeah. But that don't mean I'm going to let you start any trouble here, okay? Just be careful not to piss anyone off. And don't rip off any of the girls, got it? That's one thing I'm not going to stand for. Consider this your one warning about that."

"One thing I'd never do is steal money from a lady. You don't have to worry."

Stacklee nodded and walked away. Bluford slowly walked back to the table but decided that he was done playing cards for the night. Now it was time to buy a girl. He had enough extra money to get a nice one.

He was scanning the room for a potential whore when he saw one standing against the bar. She was tall and had the reddest hair that he had ever seen. Her breasts were average but her ass belonged to a woman twice her size. It jutted out like a balcony. She was wearing tall boots that looked like they were originally tan but were now dark brown from being caked with filth.

Walking with a confident stride, Bluford approached her and smiled.

"Good evening, miss."

The redheaded woman smiled in return. "Hello there. You looking for some company?"

"Indeed I am."

She grabbed his arm. "My name's Lily. Follow me and we can discuss the details."

The two of them went upstairs and into Lily's room. She stood in front of the bed and said, "So? What's going to tickle your fancy today?"

"To be honest, I don't know."

Lily sat down on the bed and stretched. "What about my hair? Most men who come to me seem to like my hair."

"Really?"

Running her hands through her thick red hair, Lily said, "Yeah, there was this one guy who would come by every Sunday morning asking me to choke him with it. He just loved it. He'd sit right there on the floor and I would crouch over him and lean my head over and stuff my hair down his throat while her played with his pecker."

"Well, your hair is very pretty. Can't blame the man for wanting to get closer to it." Bluford laughed. "I think I'd be interested in something like, maybe we get to screwing and you slap me, hit me a little bit, maybe scratch my face."

Lily said, "You want to get beat up a little bit? I think I can oblige. I've done that before and I'm not ashamed to say

I think I'm pretty good at it."

They discussed the price for the screw and then Bluford took out the small jar that he bought from Tom Duma. Lily looked at him strangely and said, "That's not what I think it is, is it?"

"I don't know," Bluford said. He took a swig from the jar. "What do you think it is?"

"Ass Juice?" She shook her head. "You stupid son of a bitch."

As Lily took off her clothes, Bluford felt the alcohol burning through his body like hot pins and needles. Red and brown sparks cascaded in front of him. Lily appeared to be covered in shimmering sores. Her breasts expanded until they were the size of bulging potato sacks. A dark red shell appeared over her crotch. The shell bubbled and then cracked, opening up like a flower, spilling inky darkness down Lily's legs.

Bluford rubbed his eyes. The sparks disappeared and Lily was back to normal except for a tiny patch of red tattoos above her pussy that wasn't there before. Bluford was left with a burning skull and an aching erection.

Lily climbed on top of him.

So then they got down to it, screwing furiously, starting on the bed and then moving to the floor. All through it, she slapped him in the face and hit him in the chest. He grabbed her ample ass and squeezed it which only made Lily hit him harder. When she saw that Bluford was near climaxing, she scratched him right across the face while screaming, "Take that, you filthy son of a bitch!"

Afterwards, Bluford fell asleep, his face still bleeding from the scratches and his brain still burning from the Ass Juice. Lily left the room and walked downstairs.

She said to Stacklee, "I got a man in my room, asleep. I'll wake him up when I come back. I just need some fresh air."

"That's a waste of a room."

"I'll charge him for the time. Maybe I'll get lucky and he'll stay the night and we'll get a few extra bucks out of him."

Stacklee said, "Yeah, Betty will like that."

"Be back in a few minutes," Lily said. When she got outside, she walked to the General Store. Tom Duma was stacking fruit jars on a shelf.

"Hey," Lily said.

"Lily." Tom nodded. He put one more jar away and then crouched down, reaching into a cabinet under the counter. "You need more so soon?"

"Yeah."

"These things will catch up with you someday."

"What do you care? You get your money, don't you?"

Tom shook his head. "You know I don't care much about money."

"Your wife does," Lily said.

"Don't worry about her." Tom took a black jar out of the cabinet and put it on the counter. "Here they are."

Lily put cash on the counter and picked up the jar. She unscrewed the top and poured the contents out.

"Hey! Don't do that!" Tom said.

"I just want to check them."

Out of the jar fell three green scorpions, each having two tails. Lily picked one up and held it by the head. The two tails waved as she stuck one into each of her nostrils and then sniffed deeply. The pinchers on the tails detached from the scorpion and went straight up Lily's nose.

The creature struggled to get away but failed. Lily dropped it to the floor and crushed it with her filthy boot.

Tom said, "You had to do it here? Couldn't wait till you got back?"

"Does it matter? You're getting paid either way." She put the two remaining scorpions into the jar and then walked out of the store with them. Behind her, Tom shook his head and looked over the counter at the scorpion guts on the floor. It was such a shame, an innocent little creature having to die like that.

# CHAPTER NINETEEN

Leonard looked at Clayton and thought back to when the two of them first got together. It was right before they had run into Sergio escaping from the prison camp. Leonard remembered hearing a very drunk Clayton Blood boast about his brother Jackson and how he shot four lawmen with only two bullets. How that was possible, Leonard wasn't sure. Still, he listened to the man in the donkey mask go on and on about the infamous Jackson Blood.

After most of the crowd around Clayton left, Leonard had approached him.

"So that true? You're Jackson Blood's brother?"

Clayton slammed down his shot glass. "Damn right!"

"You in the same business?"

"You asking if I'm a thief?"

Leonard smiled. "Yeah, that's what I'm asking."

From then on, the two men were like father and son though the relationship was often shaken up by Clayton's short temper and Leonard's stubbornness. The addition of Sergio to their group added a certain foundation and focus. It also helped that the new man had a plan.

Sergio had said, "There's a town in Nevada. Has a lot of gold. I know where it is and how to get it."

The prospect of a big score was enough to get Leonard and Clayton on board. Besides, the two of them had never planted any roots anywhere so traveling to the west was just as good as any other plan.

So now they were in the town of Screwhorse. Leonard was waiting on Sergio to get done with his whore so they could start preparing for the job. Clayton was smoking a cigar through his mask.

Leonard said, "You enjoy those two whores?"

"The Brady sisters? Yeah, they were fine."

"What do you think of the one Sergio picked?"

Clayton laughed. "One with the four feet? That's something new. I bet she knows a lot of little tricks."

Leonard took a sip of whiskey. "She probably spends a fortune on shoes, too."

A snort came out of Clayton's nose. "Damn right."

They sat in silence for a minute and then Leonard said, "You think Sergio's acting a little different since we came into town?"

"Different how?" Clayton said.

"I don't know. More angry. Like he's going to burst any minute."

"Didn't notice it but the man never really was a cheerful son of a bitch, you know?"

Leonard nodded. "Guess a prison camp will do that to a man."

"Sometimes it seems like he wants to talk about it and then he shuts up. I have a feeling he won't be right until he tells someone everything about his time there."

"I don't think that's ever going to happen," Leonard said. "The shit that happens in one of those camps is the kind of shit men keep locked in their hearts until they're dead and buried."

"So I probably shouldn't ask him about it, then?"

Leonard widened his eyes. "I wouldn't recommend it."

\* \* \*

Sergio had never been with a girl who had four feet and to be honest, he never thought they existed. It wasn't bad, though. She fucked like any other whore except she used her toes as if they were fingers, massaging his whole body especially his scrotum which got a lot of attention from all four of her pinky toes.

When they were done, he stood up and looked out the window. June asked him what he was looking at.

He said, "Nothing."

"You looking at the Indians?"

Sergio ignored the question.

June said, "Fine. There're plenty of windows downstairs. Why don't you go look through those, then?"

Sergio let out a heavy sigh and got dressed. He took an extra dollar out of his pocket and gave it to her. "Something extra."

June didn't respond. She just looked at him and wondered why he looked just as tense as he was before the fuck.

As he was leaving the room, Sergio said, "Be seeing you." He went downstairs and saw his two partners playing poker with a group of cowboys. Sergio stood behind Leonard and said, "Let's go."

As they got up, Clay took the money he had won. Black Boned Keith was one of the cowboys at the table and he didn't like that Clayton was leaving without giving him the chance to win his money back.

Keith said, "You best stay here and play a few more hands. I didn't come back into town just to give my money to some asshole in a jackass costume."

Clayton tilted his head. "What'd you say?"

"You heard me. Sit back down and play."

Leonard shook his head. It was a shame that young men were always so hot-headed. It always got them into trouble.

Clayton slammed his fist on the table. "Fuck you."

Black Boned Keith smiled and then drew his gun, pointing the barrel at Clayton's crotch.

As Clayton tensed up, Sergio put a hand on his shoulder and said, "Give him his money back, Clay."

"What? Now wait a minute…"

Sergio said, "Do it."

Keith lowered his gun. He watched in delight as Clayton put the money down on the table and stormed away.

"Mighty kind of you," Keith said, smiling at Sergio.

"I wasn't being kind. Just smart. I didn't want my friend to splatter your brains on the wall. That'd cause trouble for me and I don't have time for that. You have your money now so shut the fuck up." Sergio stared Keith down, not worrying about the gun being lifted again.

Leonard tapped him on the shoulder. "Let's go, Sergio." They walked out.

Outside, Clayton was standing on the porch of the brothel, the cigar still hanging out of the mouth-hole of his mask. "Shit, Sergio. Should've let me have at that bastard. You know I could've taken him, no problem."

"I know. Then the sheriff comes and locks you up. What then? Me and Leonard have to finish the job by ourselves that is if the sheriff didn't lock us up, too."

Clayton groaned. "Shit."

"You really needed that cowboy's money? After this, you'll have more gold than you know what to do with," Sergio said. "Just think of the gold."

Clayton took the cigar out of his mouth and flicked it into the street. "You're right. All that gold. I can almost taste it."

The sound of drumming echoed through the street. Sergio said, "Those Indians are making a lot of noise."

Leonard said, "Yeah and it's making me nervous. Let's go."

Before they had come to town, the three of them had decided that staying in the hotel was not a good idea. Instead, they'd set camp out behind the church alongside the small graveyard. Small town pastors usually didn't mind strangers staying near church. It provided the congregation with more souls to save. Sergio, however, had no intention of getting religion. He had a plan and God had no part of it.

\* \* \*

Maybe it was because Sergio had been emotionally distant or perhaps because she was still recovering from her sickness, but June had the urge to see the creature again.

As she was walking out of her room, her friend and fellow whore Lady Troy walked by.

"June, you feeling better?"

"Yes, guess so. I feel sick then I feel better. Then sick again," June said, slowly walking to the starfish room.

"So, I saw that man you had. He looked like an interesting one. Was he?"

"Eh, just your typical son of a bitch but he did give me some extra, though, so I guess he wasn't all bad. How's your business going?"

"I'll tell you something, June. When I first started, Betty wasn't sure about hiring someone like me. But I rarely have a free moment. You know how many cowboys are itching to see a girl with a dick? And even the men who think I'm all lady, they're pleasantly surprised when they see I'm packing a pistol, if you catch my meaning."

June laughed. "Your mouth is as dirty as a bedpan."

"And that's the way I like it!"

June shook her head and smiled. Then she slowly walked forward. "I have things to do, Troy. We'll have a drink later."

"Okay, sweetie," Lady Troy said, walking away.

As June entered the room, she saw the starfish on the ceiling. It was covered in pink webbing.

"Don't worry, baby, mommy's here," June said, climbing onto the bed to reach the starfish. As her fingers touched it, she felt the nausea strike, causing her to collapse on the floor.

"Why would you want to hurt your mommy? Why….."

# CHAPTER TWENTY

Kersey didn't bother to fetch the sheriff when Calamaro walked upstairs. He figured someone would be killed and there was no avoiding it. He still didn't tell Sheriff Doyle about that purple-bearded bastard Merrick who Calamaro had shot earlier in the day.

When he heard the explosion out front, Kersey walked to the front porch. He saw Ryan twitching on the ground with his legs all blown to bits. It was a miracle the asshole was still alive. Kersey stood there while the other two men fell to the ground and then he thought it might be a good time to get back to the front desk. He wasn't surprised. If he had been a betting man, Kersey would've put all his money on the stranger.

Calamaro came down the stairs and said, "A window broke in my room. I'll pay for it."

"Paying for the window is the least of your worries right now. Blowing the legs off one of William Lyons' boys? That'll get you dead."

"He had it coming."

Kersey shook his head. "That may be so but you don't seem to understand the situation you put yourself in."

"I think I do. If it helps any, I'll leave your hotel."

"That might be best," Kersey said. "I think I helped you enough."

"I appreciate it."

"If you appreciate it, then do me a favor and don't mention it to anyone. I don't need trouble from Lyons."

Calamaro nodded his head. "Don't worry. I won't tell anyone." Then he walked out the back door. He untied his donkey and pulled it along the area behind the buildings to keep out of sight.

Two minutes after Calamaro left, the sheriff walked into the hotel and shouted at Kersey. "Where the hell is that stranger?" He pulled his gun out.

Kersey said, "Don't know, sheriff. I fell asleep here at the front desk and only woke up when I heard the explosion. That boy okay?"

"Okay? His goddamn legs are blown off, for Christ's sake. What do you think? Now cut the shit and tell me who's upstairs."

"Just the same handful of people who've been here for weeks, sheriff."

"What about the stranger? The one that came into town today?"

Kersey shrugged. "Two strangers came in today. Which one are you talking about?"

"Whichever one blew the legs off that asshole outside."

"I guess either of them might be upstairs. I don't know but you feel free to check."

"I don't need your fucking permission," Sheriff Doyle said. He walked up the stairs slowly. He started checking every room. Half of the rooms were empty while a couple of others were being occupied by the familiar faces of men who Doyle knew weren't suspects.

He got to the room with the broken window. When he saw it was empty, he swore loudly. Then he went to the room next to it and saw the body of Merrick, his purple beard still twitching slightly.

"Fucking hell!" Sheriff Doyle walked downstairs and slammed his fists on the counter. He grabbed Kersey's shirt. "Were you going to tell me about the fucking dead man upstairs?"

"Dead man? What dead man?"

"Karl Merrick. Purple beard. Sound familiar?" Sheriff Doyle said, shaking Kersey hard. "Does it have anything to do with Nix and those assholes?"

"I don't know, sheriff. Honest."

Sheriff Doyle let go of Kersey and ran his hands through his hair. "I am seriously getting sick of this shit."

"Me, too."

"Shut the fuck up and go fetch Doctor West so he could take care of Karl. Got it?"

"Yeah, I got it."

"And if you see either of those guys, you let me know immediately. Do you understand that?"

"Sure thing, sheriff. I see the strangers, I'll let you know."

Sheriff Doyle walked out of the hotel and saw that the doctor and his sons were carrying Ryan Hickory to Doctor West's place. Chaps and Nix were able to walk on their own albeit slowly and painfully.

Doyle shouted. "Didn't Lyons tell you dumb assholes to wait?"

Nix turned and said, "Fuck you."

The sheriff shook his head. Those boys would never learn.

# CHAPTER TWENTY-ONE

Calamaro tied his donkey to a wooden cross that stuck out of the ground in the backyard of the brothel. He wondered why the man had been buried all alone back there. He walked across the cemetery with one grave and went through the back door.

Betty was at a table counting money. She spoke without looking up. "I knew you'd be coming around. Heard the explosion and just knew you had something to do with it."

Calamaro said, "That a problem? I can leave."

"No, you don't have to leave." Betty stopped counting and looked up at him. She smiled. "You're a good man. Maybe not the smartest but you have a good heart."

"I wouldn't think me a saint if I was you. Not just yet."

"What? You come here to rob me?"

Calamaro laughed. "No, I didn't come here to rob you. But don't think me some angel coming here to clean up your town. That's supposed to be the sheriff's job."

"You haven't met our sheriff, then, have you?"

"I haven't had the pleasure, no."

Betty motioned for him to follow her and he did. She brought him down a dimly lit hallway and into a small room that had been painted bright red. "Have a seat," she said.

Calamaro sat on a chair across from Betty who sat down on a well-worn Victorian couch. "Nice room," he said.

"Thank you. Everything was brought straight from

England." She patted the couch cushion as if to show him how soft it was. "You don't mind, can I ask you something?"

Calamaro nodded.

"What happened to your ear or does everyone ask you that and you're sick of answering?"

"Someone shot at it is all. There's no special story behind it."

"Was it in the war?"

"No, I didn't take a part in the war."

Betty leaned back and crossed her legs. "Most of the men who come through town either fought in the war or lie and say they fought in it. I don't remember the last time I heard a man from out of town admit he didn't fight."

"I believe it," he said. "Most men are liars."

"How about you? You a liar?"

"I'm a lot of things but not a liar. If there's something I don't want someone to know, I just keep my mouth shut."

"How does that work out?"

Calamaro smiled. "Usually just makes me look mysterious."

Betty laughed. "Well, let me ask you a question and if you want, you can stay mysterious. How about that?'

"Sounds fine."

"Where're you coming from, Calamaro?"

"Does it matter?"

"Where're you going?"

"Does that matter?"

Betty smiled and shrugged. "Guess not. Just curious, though. I've been here for a long time and so I forget what it's like in other places."

"I came from the east. The eastern coast."

"Any special reason why you left?"

Calamaro took off his hat and set it on the floor next to him. "Just decided to leave. Wasn't much left for me there."

"You don't have no family or nothing?"

"Yes," he said. "I have a family."

"You left them?"

Calamaro hesitated for a few seconds and then said, "Yes, I left them. A wife and a little girl."

Betty had been looking him right in the eye during the whole conversation but when he said this, she stared at him with more intensity. "You left your wife and child behind?"

"Yes."

"Guess I should've expected that. You know, you being a man and all."

Calamaro said, "That's another story I've told too many times."

"I'm not forcing you to tell me anything."

Calamaro grabbed his hat from the floor. "Do you have somewhere I can stay just for tonight?"

Betty stood up abruptly and adjusted her dress. "Guess you can stay in this room if you'd like. No one comes back here but me. That is, if you don't mind sleeping on the couch or the floor."

"I don't mind."

"I'll get you a blanket and some whiskey for the night. I'll bring in a bedpan, too," Betty said. "If the sheriff decides to search the place, I really can't do anything more than maybe warn you a few minutes ahead of time. Just so you know."

"A warning is more than enough."

"Well then, I'll be back in a few minutes." Betty walked out of the room, closing the door behind her. She angrily walked down the hallway and into the front of the brothel. Stacklee was tending the bar.

"Betty, you ready to take over?" he said. Stacklee hated playing bartender. Though most of the patrons didn't do anything outwardly hostile to him, they still didn't show him the proper respect. Still, at the present moment there weren't any customers so he was eager to be relieved of his duty before a crowd came in.

"Just give me a minute, will you?" Betty grabbed a bottle of whiskey and then went into the closet for a blanket. She was angry as hell but didn't want to show it to Stacklee. He'd ask what was wrong and she'd feel guilty if she didn't explain. But how could she? How could she tell him that she was disappointed that the kind-hearted stranger in town turned out to be just another lousy man who abandoned his family?

Stacklee said, "Something bothering you, Betty?"

"Don't worry about it, Stacklee."

"I always worry, you know that. It's a curse. I worry about me and I worry about you. I worry about all the girls. I thought that's why you hired me."

"I appreciate it but it's just something small and stupid."

"It about Calamaro?"

Betty stopped fiddling in the closet. "How'd you know?"

"One of the girls saw him from a window upstairs. Said he came in through the back door. He here?"

"Who said he came in?"

"Lady Troy."

Betty frowned. "I have to tell that girl to keep her mouth shut."

"So, he here or what?" Stacklee said.

"Yes, he's in the back but keep quiet about it."

"I will." Stacklee laughed. "I guess he had something to do with that explosion. Poor old Ryan Hickory lost his legs."

"It was Ryan?" Betty smiled. "I wish it were Nix."

"Me too. So what's the problem?"

"Turns out our little hero is just a typical son of a bitch. Left a wife and daughter back east and here he is in a whorehouse and he'll probably want a free one. That really sticks in my craw."

"You're angry at him leaving his wife and daughter?" Stacklee laughed.

"What the hell is so goddamned funny, Stacklee?"

"Betty, his wife and daughter are dead, killed by Union soldiers who thought they were spies. He didn't mention that?"

"No, he didn't. He said he didn't want to talk about it. Why'd he tell you?"

"Because he had too much whiskey, that's why."

Betty felt like a jack-ass but thanked her lucky stars that she hadn't yet taken her anger out on Calamaro. "I might've misjudged him, then."

"Guess you did, Betty. But if you don't mind, I'll take him the whiskey and blanket and you can watch the bar."

Betty let him do just that because she was afraid to talk to Calamaro again so soon. She knew that she was in no real position to judge considering she ran a whorehouse but it bothered her to think someone would just leave their family.

A few minutes later, Stacklee came back and said, "Calamaro wants to talk to you, Betty."

She nodded and walked back to the room. When she entered, he was lying on the couch with his feet up. His dusty boots were on the floor and his hat was over his face.

Betty said, "You taking a nap?"

"No, just resting my eyes."

"Stacklee said you wanted to talk with me."

"That's right." Calamaro took the hat off his face and sat up. "He said you got the wrong impression of me. Thought I abandoned my family. I just wanted to explain things better."

"There's no need to explain. It's your business, not mine." She didn't want to make him feel like he needed to justify himself to her. He was a grown man and whatever had happened to him and his family was none of her concern.

"I usually don't care what people think but it does bother me that you had the impression I left my wife and daughter. I opened my mouth half way so I might as well go through with it. I'd feel better. I already told Stacklee but that was only because I had too much whiskey and couldn't

103

keep my trap shut."

"You don't have to tell me anything."

"I know I don't but now I want to."

"I imagine that's something most people wouldn't want to talk about."

"That's true but you've been kind to me so I don't mind telling you," Calamaro said. He stared at the floor as he spoke. "My wife and daughter were killed by some men and since then I've just been trying to find some peace. I spend a lot of time grieving and a lot of that grieving involved me being a mean son of a bitch. But I think that part of me has passed on."

"I could see that."

"And since then, every time I'm with a woman, a whore or whatnot, I close my eyes and think of my wife. I know that sounds like a lie but it's not. I just can't bear the thought of my wife being gone so I just try to get some of those feelings back. That sounds strange, I know, screwing women while mourning my wife but that's just what I end up doing."

Betty smiled. "That's sweet in a strange sort of way."

"Guess so. I don't know. I don't imagine my wife would like it if she were alive."

"I'm sure she'd be okay with it. You'd be surprised at how understanding a woman can be."

"Maybe," Calamaro said. He stood up from the couch. "My daughter was only one years old when she was killed. That probably hurts worst of all, knowing I'll never get the chance to talk to her, have a conversation with her, get to know her, see her married and have children of her own. A child that young is still a baby, still learning about the world but now she's....."

"She's in heaven, Calamaro, don't you forget that."

"Not sure I believe in heaven, Betty. Some men shoot your wife and child, you tend to think the Lord don't care much about his flock or maybe that God died way back when and he no longer has the power to protect anybody. Why the hell would he let some bastards shoot an innocent baby that's done nothing wrong? What part of his divine plan is that? You know what my preacher said after it happened? He said that it was all God's plan to bring me back to church, bring me back to the Lord. If God thought that was going to bring me back, he can go to Hell."

Betty had expected tears to well up in his eyes when speaking about his dead wife and child but instead she saw rage.

"I can understand that," she said. "You mind if I ask? Are you out for revenge? You tracking the men who did it?"

"No." The rage in Calamaro's face subsided. "I already killed them. They were soldiers fighting for the Union. They weren't good soldiers, just men who took up arms to fight the Confederates. Hell, I don't think they even cared about the Union. I think they just wanted to shoot people."

Betty said, "I've met a lot of soldiers who are like that."

"Well, these bastards thought my wife was a spy on account she was born in Kentucky and had family there. They heard some nasty rumors about her. They shot her and when my daughter wouldn't stop crying, they shot her, too. They were stupid enough to hang around and eat the dinner that my wife had prepared for me. I came home while they were having at the food."

Calamaro took out a cigarette, lit it, and then offered one to Betty. She shook her head.

"I was lucky I had my pistol with me. I was even luckier that the bastards were worn out from eating and drinking. You should've seen their faces, all messy with food like they were pigs on a farm. I saw what they done, saw the bodies lying there two feet from where they were eating. Then I shot them all dead. I didn't have to think about it. My hand just grabbed my pistol and it was like my body was moving by itself. Bang, bang, bang. It was over that quick."

Betty walked over to the couch and sat next to him. She put her hand on his shoulder. "I'm sorry about your family and I'm sorry that I made you feel you had to explain it to me. It was none of my business."

Calamaro said, "You know, you'd think a man might feel satisfied having killed the men who killed his family. But sometimes I wish that I came to the house after they left and that I'd have to hunt them down. At least then I'd have a purpose in life, something to do, something to think about, something to accomplish. The revenge was over too quick. Too quick to make me feel any better about seeing my wife and daughter dead on the floor."

Betty put her other hand on his leg and squeezed it. She didn't intend it to be a means of seduction but that's how Calamaro took it. He grabbed the back of her head and pushed her towards him, forcing their lips to meet. Betty's tongue entered his mouth, exploring every inch of his teeth. She had always loved teeth.

She whispered. "I'm sorry about your wife." Another kiss. "I'm sorry about your daughter." Another kiss. "I'm sorry about everything." Another kiss but this one was deeper and wetter. She pulled him onto her and then felt his erection as it poked the inside of her thigh. "Close your eyes, Calamaro. Close your eyes and think of her."

He did just that as they made love on the couch and then the floor. Betty kept her eyes open, looking at this handsome man as he entered her again and again. His eyes were closed but his mouth was open just a little bit. She wanted him to feel like he was making love to his wife again not just some whorehouse madam in a dusty town. His face was beautiful, she decided, not just handsome. Even his mangled ear was beautiful. She touched it gently.

"Deeper, Calamaro, deeper," Betty said softly. "I love you." She felt him thrust deeper. "I love you." She felt him thrust deeper still. "I love you!" She felt him thrust deeper and harder while he pressed his open lips to hers, kissing and licking her.

A shout from the front of the brothel interrupted them.

"Where is he?" it said, loud and forceful. "Where the fuck is that stranger?"

Betty said, "It's the sheriff. You have to leave. Stacklee will probably be able to stall him for a few minutes but that's all."

Calamaro slowly opened his eyes and lazily rolled off her. He put his hat on first and then his boots. "Guess I'll get going, then."

"What're you going to do?"

"Guess we'll find out soon enough."

Betty pulled her dress down and stood up. "You best just leave. Just go. The next town is Keoma and it ain't that far away. You leave now he probably won't even bother you. The sheriff's pretty lazy."

"Thanks but I'd soon as just stay here and see how things work out."

"You're a stubborn son of a bitch, aren't you?"

"Yep."

Betty pushed him towards the door. "Now get! Use the back door! If you want to stay in town, fine, but don't go having a shoot-out in the middle of my place."

Betty fixed up her hair and walked towards the front hoping she'd be able to convince the sheriff to leave. She wondered how he knew that Calamaro was there. Did Lady Troy tell him? She hoped not.

Though he would have rather stayed and faced the sheriff, Calamaro walked out. He went over to his donkey and started to untie it. That's when he felt something hit the side of his head. At first he thought it was just a desert fly that flew into him but then he felt blood drip down his neck. He turned around and saw something fast coming towards his face. It was a lot bigger than a fly.

# CHAPTER TWENTY-TWO

William Lyons looked down at the unconscious Calamaro. He turned to Nix. "Help me carry this fucker and that wooden donkey out of town. I have plans for him."

They dragged Calamaro and Sartana the donkey behind the buildings, parallel to Main Street. When they reached the doctor's place, Lyons told Nix to wait while he went inside. A few minutes later, Lyons was pulling a small wagon behind him with Ryan Hickory lying in it. His legs had been blown off and the doctor did his best to bandage the stubs right above the knees. Chaps walked out behind them, limping but grinning ear to ear.

Chaps said, "Wow. That was quite an experience."

"Shut the fuck up, you piece of shit," Nix said.

"Doctor West sure works miracles. What the hell were those things the doc put on you, Ryan?" Chaps said.

"I don't know. Looked like leeches to me but bigger," Ryan said.

Chaps said, "They changed colors, too. You see that? And they smelt like honey and burning meat. I almost ate one of them."

William Lyons turned around. "Both of you. Shut the fuck up." Then he turned to Nix. "You come to me asking for help and I tell you I'll do something about it and just to wait for me and what the hell do you do? You go ahead and start more trouble. And then what happens?" He pointed at Ryan. "This asshole's legs get blown off."

Nix started gesturing with his hand, getting more aggressive than he usually would get when talking to Lyons. "We were just going to watch for him, maybe fool with him a little bit but I got anxious, know what I'm saying? You can't fault a man for that."

"You really are a stupid son of a bitch, Nix. But now you can redeem yourself. You're going to drag this cocksucker into the desert, the spot they call Cuchillo's Point. You know where it is?"

"Yeah. What do we do with that wooden thing?"

"I already told you. Bring it along." William Lyons dropped the handle to Ryan's wagon and looked at Chaps. "You can pull this asshole."

William led them out of town towards Cuchillo's Point. He never could figure out why it was called that considering it wasn't a point at all but rather a rocky area with a few shriveled trees right in the middle of the desert. He had used it plenty of times for this sort of thing and sometimes thought he should rename it. He could call it Lyons Mouth and so everyone would know that William Lyons had named it and that it was his in a way. He'd like that.

After they walked the mile and a half to Cuchillo's Point, Lyons said, "Stop here." He walked over to a rock and pulled out a small shovel. He threw it over to Nix. "Start shoveling."

Nix made a disgruntled face but when he saw William's eyes, he quickly got to digging. He dug a narrow hole five feet deep, just enough room for Calamaro's body. Lyons dumped Calamaro in there feet-first. Then he had Nix put the sand back so that only Calamaro's head was visible above the ground.

William Lyons took out a small razor from his pocket. He crouched down and then slid the blade across Calamaro's cheek several times.

"Wake up, asshole," he said.

Calamaro's eyelids started to flutter and then opened slowly.

109

Nix laughed. "Yeah, wake up!" He kicked sand into Calamaro's face. It was enjoyable seeing the guy buried up to his neck, helpless and bleeding from razor cuts. It was almost worth it getting that shot glass thrown into his eye.

Ryan banged on the side of the wagon. "Pick me up! Pick me up!" Chaps lifted him up and brought him closer to Calamaro. Ryan threw a few punches and even tried to throw a few kicks but then realized that he had no legs and so all that effort was useless. He pulled down his pants in the front and started to piss on Calamaro's head.

"Look! That woke him up!" Nix said, kicking more sand so that it mixed in with the urine.

Calamaro didn't say a word. There was no screaming, no cussing, no begging. He simply stared up at the men who surrounded him.

William Lyons put his face an inch away from Calamaro's. "You don't have anything to say? You don't want to ask us why we're doing this, why you're buried up to your neck in the desert? You're not at all wondering about that?"

The only response was a slight shaking of the head.

"It always surprises me when assholes mistake stupidity for bravery," Lyons said, putting his razor up to Calamaro's cheek again. With his other hand he grabbed some flesh and started cutting it off with the razor. He looked surprised when the man didn't scream out in pain. Calamaro simply stared at him.

The other men just hooted and hollered at the sight of William Lyons carving a piece of flesh off the guy's cheek. They found it funny that this stranger wandered into town thinking he was tough and now finding out that he was nothing but a head growing out the ground, a head that was going to be carved up like a slab of beef.

After he had a few slivers of flesh in his hand, Lyons said, "Open your mouth." He put the pieces up to Calamaro's lips but the mouth did not open.

"Open it!" Nix kicked the back of Calamaro's head.

110

That did the trick. The mouth opened and Lyons stuck the flesh in there. "Eat it," Lyons said. "Eat your skin."

The men watched as Calamaro slowly chewed his own cheek-flesh and then swallowed it. They cheered. Chaps clapped so loud that the sound seemed to echo for miles.

"How's it feel to eat your own flesh? Do you want to vomit? Go head and vomit if you want to. We'll just scoop it up and make you eat that, too. Maybe we should wait until you shit your pants and then dig you up, make you eat your own shit." Lyons said, sticking his fingers into Calamaro's mouth. "You like me sticking my fingers in there? You want to pretend my fingers are a big cock? You want to suck on them? Come on, suck, then. Suck!"

Calamaro wouldn't comply so Lyons just stuck his fingers down his throat and pulled them out violently. Then he took a flask out of his jacket pocket. It was small and silver with the inscription *To William, from your brother, Jack.*

"I guess you must need something to wash that down with, huh?" he said, unscrewing the top of the flask and holding it close to Calamaro's lips. "Open up and drink. Drink, bastard, drink!"

Calamaro opened his mouth and let Lyons pour the liquid down his throat. He swallowed as much as was poured and then closed his eyes. Lyons slapped him in the mouth. "Open your fucking eyes, asshole. You'll be dreaming soon enough." He laughed and then the other men started to laugh.

Chaps said, "What was in that flask?"

"Just something to help the man dream. Every man deserves some dreams before death," Lyons said, standing up and putting the flask back into his pocket. "I don't want him closing his eyes, though. Go get some cactus needles and make sure he can't close them."

Chaps said, "Why don't we just shoot him?"

"Because that's not fun, jack-ass. That's too easy," Lyons said. "Now get going with making sure this asshole can't close his eyes." He pointed to a lone cactus a dozen feet away. The other men walked over and got to work while he leaned against a rock. He couldn't wait until he got back home and was able get back to playing with his sons. Life was good.

Lyons smiled while the men stuck needles into Calamaro's eyelids, making sure to stick them into the flesh right above the eyes so that he'd be unable to close them. Nix, especially, was finding pleasure in the task. He made sure to stick the needles in deep and felt his erection get harder every time he did so.

Finally the job was done and they all stood around Calamaro.

William Lyons bent down and grabbed a handful of hair. "I can't promise you what you're going to see but I can promise you that you're not going to enjoy it."

Nix walked over to the wooden donkey and kicked it. "What're we going to do with this?"

Lyons shrugged.

"I think it'd be nice if we hung it from a tree, know what I'm saying?" Nix grabbed the leather reins and started pulling it to one of the barren trees. Chaps helped him hoist it up so it would hang off one of the branches. After it was hung, William Lyons took the shovel and swung it at the donkey, creating a huge crack in the side of it. He dug his hand inside and pulled something out.

Chaps said, "What the hell is that?"

"It looks like a shoe," Nix said, walking closer to Lyons.

"It's a woman's shoe." William Lyons held it up. "Why the hell would he be carrying this around?"

"Stick it in his mouth, stick it in his mouth," Ryan said. He cackled uncontrollably, watching in pleasure as Lyons did as he suggested. The heel of the shoe went right into Calamaro's mouth.

William Lyons said, "Suck on this." Then he turned to Chaps. "You have your whip with you?"

"Course I do," Chaps said. He pulled out his bullwhip and cracked it. "You want me to rough him up a bit?"

"Yeah, just a little," Lyons said. He smiled. "Give him a haircut and a shave."

Chaps laughed. With a few cracks of his whip, he tore off patches of Calamaro's hair which made both Ryan and Nix guffaw. "You got him good," Ryan said. "He looks like shredded beef!"

Then Chaps moved to the side and took off slices of flesh from underneath Calamaro's chin. The sand became soaked with blood.

"Seeing you with that whip reminds me why I keep you around," Lyons said.

Chaps laughed.

Lyons looked around. "Hey. Where's his gun?"

Ryan said, "Whose?"

"What do you mean, whose? Who the hell you think? Didn't one of you assholes think to take his gun out of his holster before we buried him?"

The three other men looked at each other but said nothing.

"Fucking idiots," Lyons said. "Let's get the hell out of here." He started walking away and Nix followed close behind. Chaps cracked his whip once more, this time an inch away from Calamaro's eyes. Then he put his whip away and started pulling Ryan's wagon.

"Don't be so rough!" Ryan said.

Chaps smiled widely, showing his huge yellow teeth.

\* \* \*

Calamaro tried closing his eyes but couldn't. He attempted to spit the shoe out of his mouth but that proved to be impossible, too. The high heel was practically down his throat. From the taste and texture of it, he knew which shoe it was.

It was the one he had gotten off that woman in Philadelphia. She had not wanted to give him the shoe at first but after he used his charm as well as some money, the woman agreed. It was a nice shoe, Calamaro thought. It still had her sweat stains on it. He thought that if he wasn't buried up to his neck with cactus needles stuck in his eyelids, he would've enjoyed having the shoe stuck in his mouth.

What worried him was that he had swallowed whatever it was that Lyons had forced down his throat. It tasted sweet and gritty like fruit juice. Calamaro knew that it wasn't an ordinary drink. His head tingled and he began seeing things, hearing things, and feeling things tickling his scalp.

There were millions of scorpions gathered in front of him, organized in lines like soldiers. It reminded him of the war and how all those boys lined up with their weapons thinking it was some sort of game that they'd walk away from. Hadn't they known that there was a better chance that they'd be killed where they stood? No, they didn't even stop to think about that. That's why he chose not to get involved. There was no honor or dignity in dying a soldier's death.

The scorpions flexed their tails, their stingers looking wet and sharp. He saw one huge scorpion in the crowd that had two tails. He thought that was strange. Whoever heard of a scorpion with two tails? Calamaro tried walking towards it but then remembered that his body was under the ground. There was no way he could move.

Then the scorpion with two tails cracked open like an egg and a tiny woman crawled out.

The woman was carrying an umbrella that rapidly changed colors. Calamaro wondered why the woman was carrying it since it wasn't even raining. Then he remembered that sometimes women carried umbrellas to protect themselves from the sun. But didn't some women carry an umbrella so they could twirl it around and catch the eyes of men?

The tiny woman stared at Calamaro and then started

114

stabbing each and every scorpion with the sharp point of her umbrella. It was a slaughter. None of the scorpions fought back, as if they were willing to die at the hand of that tiny woman who was birthed from the body of one of their brethren. Calamaro felt a tinge of sorrow for the things but knew that it was simply nature taking its course.

When the tiny woman was finished killing all of the scorpions, she stood in front of Calamaro and spoke. Her voice was high pitched like the squeaking of a wheel.

"I've never seen so many men wasted so badly," she said.

Calamaro tried to speak but the shoe prevented it.

The tiny girl spoke again. "If you save your breath I feel a man like you can manage it. And if you don't manage it, you'll die. Only slowly, very slowly, old friend."

Night came quickly and disappeared just as fast. Calamaro wasn't sure if it was the real moon or just imaginary but he watched it nonetheless. He watched as the moon became a green orb of flesh with the tiny girl sitting on top of it. Then a face appeared in the moon, the sullen face of a dying man. Its mouth opened and instead of teeth, it was filled with fiery hair. Calamaro moaned and felt as if he was about to meet his maker. Maybe God was just a giant mouth full of flaming hair underneath dying eyes and flaring nostrils. Maybe God was the one who trapped Calamaro like a living corpse in the desert as some way of praising the Holy Trinity. He remembered the preaching he had heard growing up, with all of the Amens and the Hallelujahs. All of those words floated through his mind like poisoned water.

The tiny girl on top of the moon stood up and spoke. "Hallelujah," she said. "Maybe they should call you Hallelujah."

Then she dissolved into a cloud of shimmering dust and Calamaro fell into a painful waking sleep.

# CHAPTER TWENTY-THREE

Rebecca was happy when she finally slipped into bed for the night. She had the feeling that Betty liked her and that black man Stacklee didn't seem so bad after all. As those thoughts were on her mind, she drifted off to sleep.

A noise woke her in the middle of the night.

Her eyes opened and her body froze. It was probably just one of the other girls coming up from the bar. Then the sound came again, a light knock on the door.

Rebecca said, "Who is it?" There was no answer. Was it just some drunken son of a bitch looking for a screw?

"Who is it?"

Someone whispered through the door. Rebecca could not make out what was being said so she got out of bed and tip-toed to the door. "Hello?"

The whispering got louder. There was babbling that Rebecca couldn't decipher and then the voice said, "Whore!"

Rebecca was startled by the anger in the whispering and she still couldn't tell if it was a man or a woman.

"Go away or I'm getting Stacklee." she said. "Do you hear me? Go!"

"Not until you die," the voice said. "Whore!" There was a hard bang on the door.

Rebecca jumped back and ran to her bed. The door was locked and there was no way that someone could do anything further without Stacklee or one of the other girls hearing. It was probably just some drunk. It had to be.

"Go away!" she said, expecting another angry whisper in response but there was nothing. Faint footsteps ran away from her door.

It took a while but Rebecca fell back asleep. She did so with the realization that she would probably have to get used to being harassed. Men were alike all over whether they were so-called holy men who wanted to rape young girls or the filthy cowhands who frequented the brothel. Maybe tomorrow she'd ask Stacklee for a pistol or at least a knife. After all, a lady needed some sort of protection. It was a dangerous world.

\* \* \*

After Mayor Douglas ejaculated on Ana's breasts, he looked at her face and felt like slapping the shit out of it. Stupid Mexican bitch was nothing more than a whore even though she fancied herself a dignified woman. Hell, she even considered herself an American woman. What a joke that was.

"I'm done," he said, wiping his penis on her dress. He looked down at himself. The red tattoos had spread from his penis to his bulbous belly. What the hell was happening to him? He buttoned his pants and walked back to his desk. "You can go now. I'm going to have a drink. In about twenty minutes, send in Belladonna."

Ana stared at him.

The mayor said, "You listening? That little cunt Belladonna Cardinale. Send her in."

"She's dead."

Mayor Douglas slapped his palm down on his desk. "What the fuck are you talking about?"

Ana pulled up her dress and said, "After I took her away, she passed out. Never woke up."

"The hell she did. I wasn't that rough on her."

"Well, she's dead."

"And what did you do with the body?"

"I threw it in the crow-pit like you tell me to do with all the girls."

Mayor Douglas scratched his double chin. "Shit. I really wanted another go at her. Okay, then. Well, bring me another girl. Tell my boys to go to Keoma and grab me one there. This time, tell them to get me a Chinese girl. I want something tight."

Ana ran her hands through her dark hair. "Whatever you say." She left the room, cursing the mayor under her breath. It sickened Ana to feel his scum drying on her breasts but she was intent on enduring it until she got what she wanted. Ana wanted money. She wanted power. She wanted to see Mayor Douglas choke to death on his own raggedy balls. She wanted his gold.

After Ana left the room, Mayor Douglas leaned back on his chair and puffed on a cigar. He was just about done with that Mexican bitch. As he sat there thinking about why he even took up with her in the first place, he heard footsteps outside the door. What the hell did the bitch want now? Didn't he tell her to leave? But then he heard Ana's voice coming from outside so it couldn't have been her. He looked out the window and saw her in the moonlight, hitting one of his men with a cat o' nine tails.

Then who was outside his door?

"What do you want?" Mayor Douglas said. There was no response, only the creak of the floorboards. He took a step and as he did so, a black envelope was shoved underneath the door.

Footsteps quickly disappeared down the hallway and down the stairs.

The mayor would've opened the door but he was afraid there might be a second person outside the door waiting for him. So he just bent down and picked up the black envelope.

Inside of it was a photograph.

Mayor Douglas didn't consider himself a stranger to obscenities but what was shown in the picture shocked even him. His knees weakened and he stumbled to his chair.

He brought the burning end of his cigar to the photograph. Burning it seemed like the right thing to do. He wanted to see it turn into a pile of ashes. No one else should have to lay eyes on it. But then he stopped. Though he was never superstitious, Mayor Douglas wondered if destroying the photograph would bring something even more atrocious.

So instead of burning it, the mayor shoved it face down into his wooden box full of teeth and then poured himself a drink. He hoped drunkenness would get the memory of the photograph out of his mind.

\* \* \*

A loud phlegm-filled cough woke Bluford up from a sweet, sweet sleep. It was the sweetest, most comfortable sleep he had in a long time and he was genuinely pissed off that some asshole in the next room had to cough so loudly.

Bluford saw that Lily wasn't in the bed. He sat up and rubbed his eyes, which were slowly adjusting to the darkness. He must've slept for hours and that would cost him. Stretching like a cat, Bluford sat on the edge of the bed. That's when he saw it.

A body.

Lily's body.

Even in the darkness he could see that there was lots of blood. It surrounded Lily like a deep red rug. It couldn't be real. It was a dream, it had to be.

He slowly moved his head closer and saw her wounds. Her throat had been cut so deeply that she was practically decapitated. There was another cut from the top of her breasts all the way to her crotch. Her innards were halfway out of her body. Bluford thought he could see her heart. Or it could've been her liver. He never studied medicine so he wasn't sure and he didn't want to be.

The urge to scream rose from the pit of his stomach up to his throat but he stopped it. What would people think if they caught him in the room with the corpse? There's no way they'd believe that he slept through the murder even though that was the truth. He was a stranger in town and no matter how friendly he had been to everyone he'd met, the townspeople would still view him with suspicion.

What the hell was he going to do?

Bluford wasn't just concerned about himself. He really did feel bad about Lily. She was a sweet girl even if she was just a whore. She didn't deserve to die like that. But she was dead and he couldn't help her.

He quietly got dressed and then stood by the door listening. He didn't hear a thing. The man who coughed must've fallen asleep. Bluford opened the door slowly and looked out. He didn't see anyone so he stepped into the hallway and shut the door behind him.

Bluford felt guilty leaving the corpse there but knew there was no other option. After taking a few steps down the hallway, he stopped dead in his tracks.

There was a person at the foot of the stairs.

It was too dark to see who it was. At first he thought it was Stacklee but realized that it couldn't be. Stacklee was a big guy and the person standing there was smaller. They were wearing a long coat and a hat that did a good job of casting a shadow over their face.

It looked like they were watching him. Then the figure turned and walked out of the back door.

Bluford stood and waited for what seemed like forever. He didn't know if he should just go back into the room and wait until morning. Obviously someone saw him. But what if they didn't see his face? After all, he couldn't see theirs. So maybe he did have a chance to get away.

Moving quietly, he made his way down the stairs and out the front door. He was amazed that he managed to get out so easily but didn't know where he should go next. It might be suspicious if he went up to his hotel room now. There had to be another place to stay at least until he thought it was safe.

Bluford walked down the street until he was as far away from the brothel as he thought best. He saw the church down the road and was glad to see that it appeared empty.

Once he reached it, he peered into a basement window. There were jars strewn everywhere along with piles of dark rags. He smashed the window and climbed inside. He sat down on one of the piles of rags and closed his eyes, falling asleep in minutes.

This time, however, it wasn't a sweet sleep. It was a restless one.

* * *

It had been a successful night.

The killer sat at a desk, using a razor to cut words out of newspapers and a bible. The words were arranged to spell out phrases that brought back vicious memories of childhood abuse and the witnessing of a brutal murder: mother slashing father's throat in a fit of rage. Father had not brought home enough gold so mother was not pleased. She found out about the whore he had been visiting. So mother made him lick the whore's filthy boots before she murdered them both.

From the window, the killer could see the Indians outside of town. Those goddamn heathens. The killer wished to see the redskin men torn apart by coyotes, burned alive while their penises were slowly cut from their bodies, and hung from houses like decorations. And the redskin women. They should be raped. Their breasts should be punctured with the stingers of scorpions. Their orifices should be filled with sand and teeth. They should be drowned in rivers of phlegm.

Thoughts of Lily's murder resurfaced. She had been frightened almost to death when the black-gloved hands covered her mouth and the razor glistened in the moonlight.

The killer made her sniff her own shoes before the blade destroyed her. Yes, it had been a successful night.

And tomorrow would be even better.

121

# PART TWO
## Something to Do With Death

# CHAPTER TWENTY-FOUR

Betty jumped at the sound of screaming. She had just been sitting and having her morning coffee when it happened.

Stacklee came through her door, rambling on about how Lily had been murdered and about how it was all his fault. She told him to calm down but he was too upset to stop. Finally she got him to sit down and drink some whiskey to calm his nerves while one of the girls fetched Sheriff Doyle.

When Doyle arrived, Stacklee was drunk enough to be quiet but sober enough to know that he might be under suspicion being that he was a black man working in a whorehouse full of white whores. To his surprise, it looked like the sheriff didn't even take that into consideration.

"Betty, did you see who went up with Lily last night?" Doyle said.

"Yeah, it was some guy from out of town. Came in on the stagecoach." Betty looked to Stacklee. "You talked to him, didn't you? You catch his name?"

The sheriff interrupted. "Doesn't matter what he said his name was. He probably didn't tell you his real one. Was this the same asshole who got into a ruckus with Nix and his boys?"

"No," Betty said. "It wasn't the same man. But like I told you, Stacklee talked to the guy who went with Lily."

Stacklee picked up the whiskey but thought better of it and put the bottle down. "I talked to him but he didn't seem the violent type. He was just smooth son of a bitch dressed like an Englishman."

"Well, this smooth son of a bitch cut up a whore real bad. You saw her. I almost puked up my breakfast after seeing what he done to her. Maybe Lily threatened his manhood or something and so he cut her up like a hog. I don't care why. All I care about is getting my hands on the bastard."

Betty said, "Couldn't it be one of those Indians out there?"

"No, if an Indian does something like that, they don't get sneaky about it. I don't think it was any of them. I think it was a white man."

"Did you check the hotel, sheriff?"

"If that guy is staying there, I doubt he's fool enough to be there now but I'll check anyway. Seems like your establishment is attracting the wrong sort of men. I wouldn't be surprised if the mayor closed you down."

"The mayor could go fuck himself," Betty said. She picked up the whiskey bottle and took a swig.

Sheriff Doyle started towards the door. He resisted the urge to put his hand on Stacklee's shoulder. It was a shame seeing the man fall apart like that. It was obvious that he cared about those girls.

Once outside, Sheriff Doyle walked across the street to the hotel. Just as he was about to go in, he saw Mayor Douglas coming his way.

He said, "Mayor?"

"Sheriff?"

"We have a bit of a problem. Girl was murdered last night at Betty's."

The mayor stopped, looking obviously annoyed. "So? Take care of it."

"I plan to. Just thought you'd want to know about it. She was cut up real bad. Looked like an Indian got to her," Doyle said.

"So it's an Indian did it?"

Sheriff Doyle shook his head. "No, I don't think so."

"Well, take care of it," the mayor said, walking away. The sheriff didn't know it but the mayor had bigger things on his mind like the black envelope he had received the previous day and the red tattoos that were consuming his flesh.

Once the mayor was out of earshot, Sheriff Doyle said, "What the fuck is wrong with him?" He walked into the hotel and prayed that the killer would just be sitting there waiting to be arrested. God, why couldn't it be that easy?

Betty's voice cried out from behind him. "Sheriff!"

Doyle turned around and saw the woman waving a jar in the air. He walked over to her. "What the hell now?"

"I just found this bottle under Lily's bed. It's from Tom Duma's store and one of my girls said she heard him arguing with Lily last week." Betty was shivering now. Not from the cold but from the implications.

Doyle said, "So, I'm guessing you think it's Tom Duma?"

"Maybe. It could be."

"I've known him for a long time. I've had dinner at his house. It's hard to believe he'd be capable of this."

"But it could be him, right?" Betty said. "Right?"

Doyle shook his head. "Goddamnit."

He walked away in the direction of the General Store. It was easier when he thought it was an outsider. It was difficult to accept that one of the town's own businessmen was behind the murder.

When he walked into the store, Tom Duma was rubbing his eyes with the backs of his hands. He cracked a smile when he saw Doyle. "Hi there, sheriff."

"Tom, we need to talk."

"Oh? What about?"

"About where you were last night."

The smile on Tom's face faded. "Why?"

"Make this easy on the both of us. Were you sleeping

at home last night?" he said. "The entire night?"

"Just what in the hell are you getting at? This have something to do with the ruckus over at Betty's? You know I don't visit the whores."

Sheriff Doyle put his hand on his pistol. "Just answer the question, Tom."

"I will not stand here and let you treat me like a criminal."

Doyle cocked his head. "Tom, how long we know each other?"

"I don't know. A few years."

"So we know each other fairly well. But I'm only going to ask you one more time."

Tom Duma grinded his teeth and stared at the floor. "I have things to do, sheriff," he said. "I'd appreciate it if you left my store."

Doyle shook his head. He took two steps forward and grabbed Tom's arm, flinging him to the floor. Then he took him by the collar and dragged him outside. "You have to learn to cooperate, Tom. I don't have time for bullshit."

At first, Tom Duma kicked and screamed as he was being dragged across the street to the jail. Then he quickly stopped and decided that it would be in his best interest to shut his goddamn mouth and let things work naturally.

"In you go," the sheriff said, as he opened the door to the cell and pushed Tom into it. "You want, I'll let your wife know where you are."

"No need," Tom said. "I saw her watching from the window. She knows exactly where I am."

# CHAPTER TWENTY-FIVE

When Mary woke up, she saw Timothy Horn lying on the floor, covered in squid-guts and semen.

The night had been a dreamlike orgy of smelly wet sex and Timothy's nonsensical babbling. Mary didn't understand most of what he had said. He had talked about a furry, black toad that was the size of a man and how it was behind the assassination of President Lincoln and all other political killings. Mary simply nodded and feigned interest as he went on about how the toad fashioned bullets out of black goo.

After giving his lecture, Timothy forced her to the floor several times and made her lick the squid-stained wood. Then he let Mary fall asleep only to wake her minutes later with more babbling and more disgusting requests.

Finally he fell asleep and Mary was able to get some shuteye only to awake at dawn at the first sound of commotion in the brothel.

So as she sat there looking down at the crazy son of a bitch on the floor, Mary fantasized about getting up, putting on her fancy boots, and stepping on his throat until she felt the floor through the sole of her boot.

Instead of doing that, however, she found herself staring at the squid-parts that were now scattered around the room. It was strange how they seemed to glow in the sunlight.

Timothy let out a low rumble of snores and then Mary put her head on the pillow, still staring at the fishy mess and still wondering just how she could go about killing Timothy Horn.

\* \* \*

Bluford was surprised that he was able to sleep through the night in the church basement. When he opened his eyes, he was staring at the ceiling. At first he thought about trying to catch the next stagecoach but knew that he'd probably be caught before he made it to the next stop. Then he entertained the idea of trekking through the desert on his own but realized that he was the last person to be fit for survival in such a harsh environment.

So Bluford decided on going to the hotel to get his things and taking it from there. He crawled out of the basement window and started running until he reached the alley next to the hotel. When he got up to his room, Bluford opened the door and saw a very drunk Stacklee sitting on the bed.

Shit.

"Oh," Bluford said. He knew he was dead meat. Stacklee must have found out about the body, gotten drunk, and was now planning to beat the shit out of Bluford.

Stacklee stood up.

Bluford put his hands up. "I know what you're thinking but you have to believe me. I didn't kill that girl!"

"Didn't think you did."

Bluford squinted. "What?"

"I'm usually pretty good at knowing what a man's capable of and you didn't look like a man who would cut up a girl like that," Stacklee said. Tears filled his eyes. "Not saying I'm entirely sure. Could be you're crazy but to tell you the truth, I have a suspicion it's someone else."

"Who? Who would do that?"

"Timothy Horn, the mayor's nephew. But I don't know for sure," Stacklee said. "Where've you been?"

"The church basement."

He was interrupted by the door being kicked open and

Sheriff Doyle pointing a gun at him.

"Hands up, asshole," Doyle said, watching as Bluford complied. "Stacklee, I'm surprised to see you here. You helping him escape? You know very well this here might be the killer. Hell, he could've killed you for Christ's sake."

Stacklee said, "I don't think he's the one, sheriff, but if you feel you have to take him in, well, then I guess that's what you have to do."

"I locked Tom Duma up, too, Stack," he said. "I'll get to the bottom of it and if your friend here didn't do it, well, then you two will be playing marbles in no time."

Doyle hoped he could solve the crime with no problems. He reckoned it was one of the two men he was locking up or perhaps a drifter who was long gone. Either way, he wanted to be done with it.

So he brought Bluford to the jail and put him in with Tom Duma. Doyle looked at both men and thought that maybe they'd both hang themselves. Yeah, that'd make his job a hell of a lot easier.

\* \* \*

Despite Bluford's career path, he had never actually been in jail before. He was that good of a con man. So it was hard for him to grasp the concept that he might be hanged in the morning.

He was surprised he was sharing a cell with such an unassuming man, the proprietor of the General Store. That made Bluford feel a little better. At least the sheriff was open to the possibility that someone other than Bluford did it.

Tom Duma said, "So you drink that Ass Juice yet?"

"Yeah."

Tom laughed. "How'd you like it?"

"I don't know."

Tom laughed again, a low chuckle that echoed through the small cell.

Bluford didn't find the situation at all funny so he just faked a soft laugh and sat down. They both were silent and lethargic for a while, knowing that all they could do was wait until the sheriff finished his investigation.

But then Tom started pacing back and forth, biting his nails and mumbling. "There's got to be something else. Something. I know there has to be."

Bluford said, "Hey. You okay?"

"What? Oh, yeah. I'm fine."

"Okay then." Bluford said.

Tom stopped pacing and said, "You ever been with a whore?"

"Uh, yes, I have," Bluford said. "Why?"

"See, I never could see the draw to it. You go in there and fuck one of those whores and you pull your pecker out and think that she has a nice wet pussy but you may just be dipping your pecker in some other man's seed. Doesn't seem right to me."

"I guess that's something to think about."

Tom stood up. "Doesn't that seem disgusting to you? The way I see it, a man should just find himself a good virgin and if he can't find a virgin, get a woman who isn't so worn out. Then he could clean her up and make sure she doesn't screw around on him."

Bluford said, "Yeah, I suppose that's so."

"See, I have a wife and she treats me pretty good when she's not raising hell, hollering at me and all that. But when we go to bed, well, that's when the fun starts."

"Sir, I hardly think your wife would appreciate this conversation."

"She's not here, now," Tom said. "Is she?"

Bluford shook his head. "No, she isn't."

"You know what I like doing? I like lying on the floor and having my wife piss on my face. That's not so strange in this town. I know what goes on there at Betty's place and I know the girls do worse than that."

"I didn't say it was strange. I didn't say anything."

130

"Well, I could see by the look on your face that you're getting uncomfortable. But I do have a point. I'm not just jawing your ear off for no reason. I'm just saying that even though my wife can be a rough bitch on occasion, I still enjoy choking on her piss. Get it?"

Bluford said, "I guess so."

"It's good for the skin, too. The piss, I mean. Look." Tom put his hands on his face and walked close to Bluford. "Look at my skin. See how nice and smooth it is? That's from my wife's piss. That's something, huh?"

"Yeah, that's something." Bluford wasn't sure what sort of reaction Tom was expecting. Why was he talking about the disgustingly intimate details of sex acts with his wife? Was the man looking for Bluford to be sickened or excited by it? Perhaps the man wanted to find someone who shared the same desires. Still, it was a strange thing to talk about. It seemed so out of place.

"So, you been up to Betty's place yet?" Tom said.

"Yeah."

"Get yourself a girl?"

"Yeah."

Tom said, "Which one?"

Bluford's stomach churned when he thought of the eviscerated corpse. "Lily."

"Well, I'll be damned." Tom went back to the wall and leaned on it. He stared at the floor and fell silent for several minutes. Then he said, "So was she good?"

Bluford hesitated. "Who?"

"Lily," Tom said. "Was she a good fuck?"

"Jesus Christ." Bluford walked to the other side of the cell and sat down. He didn't want to talk anymore unless it could help prove his innocence. As he sat there in silence, Bluford found himself staring at Tom Duma's face and in particular, his skin. Did his wife's urine really work wonders like the man had claimed? He didn't know but thought that if he did get out of the town alive, maybe he'd try it.

# CHAPTER TWENTY-SIX

Lady Troy was busy dancing in front of the mirror as was her morning routine, caressing her breasts while her penis swung back and forth, back and forth. She didn't hear the noise coming from the other rooms in the brothel. She didn't know that Lily had been found murdered. Instead, she danced and read a little bit out of a book that a young Frenchman brought her. It was written by a man named De Sade and it aroused Lady Troy greatly. Reading was much more fun than hanging around with the other whores. They were so needy and weak. She didn't need them. After all, she had her book.

She was so engrossed in that book that she did not see the door open or see the razor shine in the sunlight as the black-gloved killer rushed forward. She did not see death as it came up from behind.

The killer slashed her across the neck and grabbed her hair, shoving her face down deep into her chamber pot, the blood from her wound leaking into it. She coughed on a mouthful of her own piss. The killer pulled Lady Troy's head up, giving her a moment to take a breath right before her head was shoved back in. Her mouth was open as it went down into the slop and chunks of flaky shit sloshed down her throat. Finally, she succumbed to a filthy death.

The killer left the room, giggling.

* * *

After she heard about the murder, Rebecca Bywater was afraid for her life. It hadn't been just a drunk harassing her the night before. It must've been the killer.

She drank a half bottle of whiskey and sat on her bed. In her drunken haze, she took out the medicine that the man from the General Store had given her. He had said it was for her woman parts. It was probably pretty common for whores to get problems down in that region and come to think of it, Rebecca did feel itchy down there.

She took out the small sack of black paper and started to unwrap it. Inside was bright blue goo. It wasn't like any medicine she'd ever seen but if that Tom Duma fellow was a trusted member of the town, it must be fine.

So Rebecca rubbed the goo all over her vagina and leaned back on her bed. In minutes she felt the itching go away while her pubic area pulsed with each heartbeat. Then she felt feverish. Something was wrong. She sat up and looked down at her crotch.

Tiny blue crabs were running out of her vagina.

She jumped off her bed, screaming and swatting at the crabs. In her confusion and horror, she didn't see when the window opened. She didn't see the razor glistening in black-gloved hands as the killer crept closer to her.

Rebecca's legs were now bright blue from the tiny creatures crawling all over her. The killer grabbed her by the hair and sliced her throat. Blood splashed down onto Rebecca's legs, drowning the crabs. The razor slashed again but this time from her chest down to her pubic hair causing her insides to spill out onto the dull brown rug.

The killer looked at the mess and inhaled the stench.

Death smelled good.

# CHAPTER TWENTY-SEVEN

Betty Black heard one of her girls say that William Lyons and his boys knocked Calamaro out and took him out into the desert.

It couldn't be true, she thought. Calamaro didn't seem the kind of man to be caught off-guard. He seemed to be a strong man with good instincts. Maybe the girl got it wrong. Maybe it wasn't Calamaro.

Stacklee said, "I checked with Angie. She described him and it's Calamaro alright." He had his head down, not wanting to look her in the eyes when he told her the bad news.

"Maybe Angie got it wrong."

"No, I don't think she did."

Betty was still surprised that she cared so much about the stranger. Normally she didn't give a shit about the men who passed through. For some reason Calamaro touched her heart in a way that she hadn't been familiar with for a long time.

Stacklee said, "You want me to go find him?"

"And then what? You think Lyons is just going to hand him over? Him and his boys would kill you, you know that. And don't you want to find out who killed Lily?"

"The sheriff is taking care of that. Already locked up Tom Duma and that card cheat Bluford."

"You think he did it? The card cheat, I mean."

"No, I don't think so," Stacklee said. "But right now the least I could do is try to save Calamaro before he's killed, too." He knew it would be a stupid decision but he was prepared to make it. It wasn't often that a white man stuck up for him and he had appreciated that. "I'll be careful. Sneak around some, maybe do some long distance shooting."

Betty said, "You don't even know how many there are. Do you?"

"Angie wasn't clear on that. Maybe four or five including William himself."

"Well, if that's what you think you should do, I'm not going to stop you."

Stacklee walked to the closet and pulled out a shotgun and a rifle. "I can make due with these. If I think I can't handle it, I'll come back, Betty, I promise."

"You best do that. I don't need to go to two funerals."

"Well, if Lyons gets a hold of me, there'll probably be nothing left to bury," Stacklee said. He regretted it the second it came out of his mouth. "Sorry, Betty."

"Just do what you have to do," she said and then walked away.

* * *

When the sun appeared, Calamaro's eyes burned.

Through the burning, he saw a woman on the horizon, her dress blowing in the early desert wind. At first he thought he was witnessing the return of the tiny woman. He thought she was coming to destroy him just like she destroyed all those scorpions. But then he saw that the woman on the horizon was not carrying an umbrella. She was carrying a shovel.

Calamaro felt like his eyes and mind were the only parts of his body that still functioned. He couldn't even tell if he still had any arms and legs. Perhaps there were underground insects that fed on human flesh and bone. They might chew on his neck, severing his head from his body. Then maybe a hawk would swoop down, grab him by the hair, and take his head up into the sky.

The woman on the horizon got closer, her dress swaying in the wind even more. Was she going to come and bury the dead scorpions? But he looked around and realized that all the insects were gone.

Dust settled in his ears.

Through the dust he heard the muffled footsteps as the woman walked nearer. Then a voice said, "You will be out soon."

Calamaro was surprised. It wasn't a woman at all. It was a man. An Indian man.

"Be calm," the voice said again. When the man reached him, he stuck his shovel in the ground inches away from Calamaro's face. The Indian bent down and gently took the shoe from his mouth. Then he pulled a buffalo bladder full of water that hung from his shoulder and put it to Calamaro's lips. "Drink," he said.

The water was warm but refreshing. Once his mouth and throat were satisfied, Calamaro paid more attention to the Indian who was using his shovel to dig him out.

He wore a purple dress and make-up just like the whores in town. Calamaro had heard about men who dressed like women but had never seen one himself.

"Getting you out soon, friend," the Indian said. With great effort, he continued to dig until he finally put the shovel down and pulled Calamaro out of the hole. For a tall, lanky Indian man wearing a dress, he was quite strong.

Once he was out of the hole completely, Calamaro tried standing up but found that his legs simply wouldn't hold his weight. He collapsed into the arms of the Indian and passed out with the smell of white sage creeping up his nose.

* * *

In the distance, Stacklee saw a woman digging. Next to her was a familiar head on the ground and Stacklee grunted in disgust. Did those bastards cut off Calamaro's head?

But then he saw the head move.

Stacklee slowly walked forward, keeping the rifle poised and ready just in case. As he got nearer, he saw that the woman with the shovel wasn't a woman and that the head in the ground was Calamaro's.

When he was a hundred yards away, Stacklee aimed his gun at the man in the dress. He'd be damned if he let someone bury Calamaro alive. But then he saw the man in the dress pull Calamaro up out of the hole. He wasn't burying him, he was digging him up.

Stacklee slowly approached them and when he did, he saw Calamaro collapse into the man's arms. He kept his gun ready. Then he said, "Hey."

The Indian looked at him but said nothing. When he saw the gun, he nodded slowly.

Stacklee took a step closer. "I said hey."

Again there was no response so he pointed the gun at the Indian who finally said, "I heard you."

"What're you doing with him?"

"I dug him out. Some men put him into the ground," the Indian said. His voice was soft and feminine.

Stacklee said, "What business is it of yours? Who are you?"

"Kimama."

"You know him?" He gestured towards Calamaro who was unconscious.

"No, I do not," Kimama said. "You do?"

"Yes." Stacklee walked closer and kept his gun pointed at the Indian.

"I mean no harm." Kimama said.

Calamaro moaned. His legs straightened as he tried to stand on his own. He looked up and saw the Indian holding him. Then he looked in Stacklee's direction. With a gravelly voice he said, "Stacklee?"

"Yeah, it's me." He pointed the gun to the ground and walked over. "Those bastards really did you in, huh?"

Calamaro tried smiling but groaned in pain instead. His cheeks were raw and bloody. "Not as bad as it looks." He straightened his legs again and found that he was able to stand up on his own. Kimama gently let go of him.

Calamaro coughed, clearing the dust from his throat. The dust blew out of his mouth and out the wounds in his face. He looked at Kimama and said, "Thank you."

"You do not have to thank me," the Indian said.

Stacklee was still apprehensive about putting his guard down despite the Indian having saved Calamaro's life. He said, "Where's the rest of your tribe?"

Kimama gave a sly grin and shook his head. "I belong to no tribe. Not anymore."

"How's that?"

"I was told to leave."

"You with those Indians that are making camp outside of Screwhorse?"

Kimama frowned. "No. Not them. My people are many, many miles away."

"I hope so," Stacklee said. "Why you wearing a dress?"

"I am both a man and a woman."

Stacklee squinted. "The hell you say?"

"Sometimes when a baby is born, the gods put two spirits into its body. One man spirit and one woman spirit. In my tribe, those who have two spirits have two choices. They may dig the graves for the dead or they may tell the fortune of the living. I have chosen to do both." He picked up his shovel and put it over his shoulder. "I like to keep busy."

Calamaro was next to him, wobbly on his feet. With painful effort he spoke.

"I'm going back to town."

Stacklee shook his head. "That would be foolish as

hell and you know it. You know those boys will finish the job. You best just count your blessings and continue on your way." He looked down at the ground. "A lot of shit's going on. One of the girls was killed. Real bad. I imagine if you come back to town, the sheriff will lock you up, too. Already locked up Tom Duma and that stranger who dresses like an Englishman."

Calamaro said, "I'm not going away."

"You understand you're lucky? Lyons could've put a bullet in your head. You could be dead. You think it's smart to give him the chance to kill you again?"

Kimama started walking away.

Stacklee said, "Where you going?"

The Indian didn't turn around when he spoke. He simply stopped walking and said, "I am going on my way. Your friend is welcome to join me while his body heals." Then he continued on.

Calamaro thought about his options. He was fearful of Indians but this one had saved his life. He walked over to the tree where his donkey was hung and untied it. Then he followed Kimama, dragging the donkey behind him in the sand.

"I'm just leaving to heal for a while. I'll be coming back," Calamaro said.

With a frustrated grunt, Stacklee followed them. As they walked, he looked at Calamaro's wooden donkey.

"Where'd you get that?"

"Why?"

"Just wondering is all. Not everyday you see someone dragging something like that across the desert."

Calamaro said, "After what happened to my wife and daughter, I started traveling, going nowhere in particular. I traveled westward and came across an abandoned Union prison camp. It was full of corpses."

"That's not so strange," Stacklee said. "A lot of people die in those types of camps."

"It wasn't just that there were corpses. I mean there were bodies of men torn up like wild animals ate them or something. Skulls smashed, some skulls made into soup bowls. Fingers and toes all in piles. I think there was even a Union flag made of skin. It was as if the soldiers had tortured and killed all the prisoners once they found out the war was over."

Stacklee said, "That's crazy."

"Yeah. I walked through the whole prison camp feeling like I was drunk or feverish, seeing things that weren't there. I went inside one of the little buildings, I guess it was a room for the officers or something, and I saw this wooden donkey sitting next to a table with a plate of human toes right in front of him as if that was his supper. He even had a cap on, if you could believe it. The cap looked like it had been through battle and it had the name Sartana sewn into it so that's what I call him. Sartana."

"Where's the cap?"

"I didn't take it. I figured he don't need it being he's made of wood and all."

Stacklee looked at the hole in the side of the donkey. "Looks like there's stuff in there."

"There is."

"What?"

"Just some things. Some of the things I picked up along the way," Calamaro said, pulling the leather reins so hard that his wrists and palms were bleeding again.

"I see shoes. Lady shoes."

"Yeah, there're some in there."

Stacklee tried not to smile but he couldn't resist. "You wear them?"

Calamaro laughed. "No, I don't wear them."

"Then who does? You give them to ladies to wear?"

"Most of them aren't for wearing."

"What do you mean?" Stacklee said.

Calamaro stopped and pulled one of the shoes out. It had a blade attached to its heel. "This is what I mean."

Stacklee nodded.

Up ahead of them, Kimama stopped and pointed to a group of boulders forty yards ahead. "That is where we will stay. It is a good place to hide, a lot of small places that cannot be seen."

When they got there, Kimama made a soft spot out of desert weeds for Calamaro. "You can rest here. I will prepare some medicine for you." He started digging in the pouch that hung around his neck.

Stacklee said, "I'm not going to stay long. Betty'll be worried sick."

"Do me a favor, Stacklee," Calamaro said. "Don't tell anyone else I'm alive. I guess you could tell Betty but make sure no one else finds out, not even any of those whores. Lyons and the others find out I'm alive they'll have time to prepare and they're likely to take out their anger on you and Betty. Understand?"

"I do." Stacklee left for town. The other two men were alone among the boulders. Calamaro asked if he would be willing to help in getting vengeance on the men who buried him alive. The Indian agreed.

After they had a plan, Kimama handed over a handful of crushed herbs. "Swallow this."

Calamaro looked at the medicine the Indian had prepared and thought it looked like something a man would vomit. Still, he figured that Kimama probably knew what he was doing. It was unlikely that he would be trying to kill Calamaro since he had already saved his life. He swallowed the herbs and then felt heat well up in his chest.

Kimama said, "You will feel many things. It is okay. Just close your eyes. If you feel scorpions on your skin, do not be afraid. That is how it works."

For the next hour, Calamaro was in and out of delirium.

He decided to put all of his trust in the Indian and fought the fear that came when he felt scorpions pinching his skin. He smelt burning flesh and the musky scent of an unwashed woman. There were sounds, too, like the chattering of many teeth and the low roaring of a steam engine.

Then he felt a hand on his forehead and assumed it was Kimama's but when he opened his eyes, he saw the Indian sitting ten feet away. Calamaro closed his eyes again and was lulled into sleep by the sound of high heels clip-clopping around him.

He saw his wife and daughter dead on the floor of his house. Their killers were seated at the table, eating and drinking. He looked at the men. Every single one of them looked like William Lyons.

One of the killers looked over and said, "That your family? We sure did enjoy killing them. Especially your wife. We even stuck our fingers in her holes to see what we'd find. Sometimes there's treasure in there. This time there was just some dead scorpions inside your wife's ass. How about that?" The killer took a bite of food. "She's worthless but makes a mighty good meal."

Rage surged through Calamaro's body. He tried reaching for his pistol but it wasn't there. The men at the table continued to eat while the bodies of his wife and daughter were melting into blue puddles filled with tiny crabs.

Calamaro felt himself running from the house, running from the men who all looked like William Lyons. He vowed he'd come back and get revenge on the killers of his family. He would come back and slaughter them all.

# CHAPTER TWENTY-EIGHT

"So, he's okay?" Betty said.

"Well, he's alive." Stacklee had told her the whole story about Calamaro. "I wouldn't say the man's okay physically or even mentally. The man's got a lot of healing to do."

Betty said, "I guess he'll just have to …"

There was a scream from upstairs. It was Angie.

Betty ran up to her room and found her crying on the hallway floor. She pointed down the hall. "It's the new girl."

"Who? Rebecca?" Betty said. Angie nodded.

Betty slowly opened the door. In the middle of the floor was Rebecca's body lying in a pool of blood and intestines. Her throat had been cut and her body sliced open.

Betty started to cry. Within the last twenty-four hours two of her girls had been murdered. Calamaro was abducted and most likely dead. It was all too much for her.

Then there was another scream. This time it was Stacklee saying that Lady Troy was dead, too. Her killer had cut her throat and left her face-down in the chamber pot.

"Angie, when was the last time you talked to Lady Troy?" Betty said.

"Yesterday. But I heard her singing this morning. She was fine."

"Go tell the sheriff two more girls are dead," Betty said. "Stacklee, get all the girls out of their rooms."

Stacklee nodded.

Angie broke down, sobbing like a wounded child. "Who could have done something like that? I can't….." She stomped downstairs and left the brothel.

When Angie walked into the jail, Sheriff Doyle was leaning up against the wall, smoking a cigar. He looked worn out.

"Sheriff," she said. "Two more girls are dead!"

"You have to be fucking kidding me." Sheriff Doyle slammed his fist against the wall. Was the shit storm never going to end? He grabbed his hat and headed for the door.

As he was walking out, he bumped into Mrs. Duma.

"I'm here to see my husband, sheriff," she said.

"That right? Well, it's his lucky day."

"Why's that?"

Doyle didn't answer. He just grabbed his keys and led her to the jail cell. Though he was always polite to the woman, something about her irked him. She was just too bitchy for his taste. How Tom Duma lived with her and didn't put a bullet in his head was beyond him.

* * *

Bluford Barnes had just closed his eyes when he heard the sheriff walk in with Tom's wife strutting in behind him. She was an intense and bitter-looking woman but attractive, very attractive. Bluford thought that under different circumstances, he might like to make a try at her. She looked like she'd enjoy a good, hard screw.

Mrs. Duma handed her husband his coat and hat. Something in Bluford's mind clicked. There was something wrong. But what? Then he saw it.

The coat. The hat.

Bluford froze. In his mind he saw the shadowy person at the bottom of the stairs and it became clear that it was the same man who was now getting freed from the jail cell.

Tom Duma put his hat on and then turned to the sheriff.

144

"No hard feelings. I know you were doing your job."

Sheriff Doyle nodded. "Just make sure you cooperate next time."

As Tom Duma put his coat on, he started to cough. It was a thick, loud phlegm-filled cough that was instantly familiar to Bluford. It was the same one that woke him up right before he discovered Lily's body.

And now the sheriff was shaking hands with Tom. Bluford's throat constricted, nausea creeping through his body. He watched the killer leave with his wife.

The sheriff looked back at Bluford.

"You going or what?" the sheriff said.

Bluford didn't answer. He simply ran out of the cell.

# CHAPTER TWENTY-NINE

Betty was looking at a walking corpse.

Or at least that's what she first thought. The man who walked through the doorway was bloody, his face mutilated beyond recognition. His body was covered in thick dust.

"Oh my God," Betty said, dropping the glass of whiskey she was drinking from. It shattered at her feet, splashing alcohol all over her boots.

The walking corpse smiled and said, "So. How do I look?"

It was Calamaro.

Betty laughed through her tears. It was amazing how this man who had just gone through hell managed to show a sense of humor. But she knew that it was only for her sake, so that she didn't break down completely. Calamaro was no doubt suffering both physically and mentally.

Betty came out from the back of the bar and ran up to him, wrapping her arms so tight around Calamaro that he grunted in pain. She let go but then placed her hand on the small of his back.

From behind Betty, Stacklee walked downstairs. He said, "So, looks like the Indian knew what he was doing. You managed to walk back to town okay."

"I don't feel as shitty as I look," Calamaro said. "I feel like I took a bad fall off a horse. But I imagine my face looks pretty bad."

"Well, it doesn't look good."

Calamaro laughed and when he did, blood and drool seeped out of the gashes in his face. Betty pulled a handkerchief from her brassiere and wiped his face. She turned to Stacklee. "Did you tell all the girls to leave?"

"All of them but Mary and June," he said. "June said she wanted to stay and being she was sick, I didn't want to argue. I thought we'd take turns watching her. And Mary still has Timothy Horn in there. She said he's been out cold for a few hours. Man wore himself out."

Betty said, "Well, I still don't feel safe with them up there."

"As long as we're done here, no one's getting in." Stacklee turned to Calamaro. "And I found out from Kersey that Nix and his boys are up in your room at the hotel."

"Did you tell him to take his customers and clear out?"

"Yeah."

"Did he give you any trouble about it?"

Stacklee said, "Who? Kersey? No, he knows something's going to happen whether he likes it or not."

Betty grabbed Calamaro's shoulder. "Don't do this."

"You know damn well I'm not going to change my mind." He put his hand on hers. "But I appreciate you trying to stop me."

Kimama walked in through the back door, dragging his shovel. He said, "The man named Lyons. He is in his house."

"Good," Calamaro said.

"He has a family. Wife. Small boys. You think this is a good idea?"

"Long as the wife doesn't pull a gun, she'll be left alone. The boys won't try nothing."

Their conversation was interrupted by a scream from upstairs. Betty said, "That's June! I knew you should've made her come down!"

Stacklee said, "Like I said, she told me she wanted to stay."

Betty shook her head and ran up the stairs. The others followed.

They found June on the floor, a starfish on her chest, two of its arms hooked on her areolas. Her eyes were opened but they were glazed over with blue goo.

Stacklee bent down and held her in his arms. Her legs shook, the four feet trembling like branches on a tree. All twenty toes wiggled.

Kimama slowly bent down in front of her. She looked at Betty. "May I help?"

She nodded.

Rubbing his hands together, Kimama chanted softly. He stuck his fingers into his mouth and massaged his teeth. He lifted up June's calves and put her feet to his lips, taking all twenty, wiggling toes into his mouth.

The others watched as Kimama sucked on June's toes, slurping loudly, drool oozing down his chin and onto the floor. The girl didn't seem to mind. In fact, it looked like her eyes were becoming less glazed. Kimama was healing her.

Stacklee thought it was strange seeing the dress-wearing Indian brave sucking on a whore's toes. After three minutes of it, June's eyes were back to normal and she sat up on her own. "What happened?" she said, looking down at her chest and seeing the starfish attached to her.

Kimama pulled her toes out of his mouth. He yanked the starfish off June's chest. She yelped in pain. Her areolas were covered in deep red tattoos.

The Indian held up the creature and then slammed it down onto the floor, killing it.

"Why'd you do that?" June said. "It was my baby."

"This creature is not a good creature."

Calamaro walked over to the window and looked out to see if there was any sign of trouble. There was a small

148

crowd gathering by the hotel and he could see the sheriff standing there trying to calm the crowd. He didn't seem too concerned and Calamaro could tell that the man would rather be somewhere else.

He turned away from the window and said, "Stacklee, let's leave through the back and head up to the hotel now. I'll go get Sartana. Then Kimama, you meet me up by Lyons' house."

The Indian nodded.

Stacklee said, "Hope the plan works."

"It will," Calamaro said. "But if it doesn't, it was nice knowing you."

* * *

Nix walked into Calamaro's hotel room. He thought it was real funny having some fun in that dead bastard's bed. As he entered, he saw Chaps and Ryan under the covers. He said, "One of the whores just told me that Stacklee and Betty found out about Calamaro."

"Isn't that something? I wished I could've seen that nigger's face when he found out," Ryan said.

Nix scoffed. "Man, you should never wish to see a nigger's face. That's bad luck."

Ryan laughed hysterically while Nix joined him in bed. After they had gotten back from dealing with Calamaro, Chaps finally got the courage to share his feelings with Nix. One thing led to another and soon he was wearing a dress and was sucking on Nix's tiny pecker. Ryan watched the whole thing while he pleasured himself. His leg stumps looked like two extra penises and so both Nix and Chaps sucked on them a little bit.

Chaps said, "Nix, you want me on my stomach? I can take it."

"Maybe later. A man needs time to recover, know

what I'm saying?"

Nix was glad that the three of them were finally honest with their desires. He hated having to pretend he was interested in pussy. When he flexed his muscles around town, he had really wanted to impress the men not the women. Chaps was perfect. The guy didn't have a macho bone in his body so there was no risk of the two of them battling for male supremacy.

Nix said, "Right now I'd like just to take a load off, relax, maybe play some cards. I don't know about you two but I've been dreaming about poker, know what I'm saying?"

"Sure thing. Cards sound good," Ryan said. "Did you ask Kersey about those cards from France? The ones with the pictures of a woman and a snake."

"Kersey wasn't there."

"What?"

"He wasn't downstairs. Didn't see anyone down there at all."

Ryan squinted. "That's weird, don't you think?"

"Yeah and this place has been awfully quiet. I could've sworn when we got in all the rooms had been taken up," Chaps said, adjusting his dress.

Nix scratched his head. "Maybe there's a picnic we don't know about."

Before Chaps or Ryan could reply, a shotgun blast came through the wall. Ryan was hit in the groin. He screamed and fell off the bed onto his leg stumps. Another blast came through and hit Nix in the legs. He fell to the ground and screamed, "Shit!"

Chaps reached for his bullwhip. He yelled, "Stop your shooting!"

Because he expected a response in the form of a shotgun blast, Chaps was surprised when he heard a voice coming from a hole in the wall.

"Any of you religious men?"

Chaps and Nix looked at each other. They recognized

the voice but were shocked to hear it.

Again, it said, "I asked if any of you are religious men?"

Ryan was trembling on the floor. He slid his hand underneath the bed and pulled out a starfish. It squirmed in his hands. Ryan rolled over onto his stomach. Blood started to spread out like a rug underneath him. The starfish squirmed out of his hands and floated on the puddle.

"Where the hell'd you get that?" Nix said.

"Found a barrel of them in the church about a week ago."

Another blast through the wall but this time it didn't hit anyone. Again the voice spoke through the hole. "Though I don't think it'd be much good for anyone, you should probably start praying if you believe in that sort of thing."

Nix looked at Ryan. "There's no way that fucker survived, know what I'm saying?"

Ryan shook his head slowly. "Guess he did, Nix, but look at me. I'm not going to survive. I feel like a slaughtered pig." His large eyes got even larger as they bugged out of his head. "Things are starting to look blurry, blue. You look like a donkey. Are you wearing a mask or something? A costume? Oh, lord, my head hurts."

Nix knew Ryan would be gone in a minute or two. There was no use in trying to help the bastard. He looked at Chaps who appeared to be in deep thought.

"Is that you, Calamaro?" Chaps said.

"It just might be," the voice answered. "I think it'd be best if your friend Nix came on out in the hallway."

Nix shook his head. His legs were busted up badly but he thought he could probably make it if he ignored the pain. "I'm coming out!" He figured there was no harm in dragging himself to the hallway if he was armed so he grabbed his pistol and started crawling.

When Nix reached the door, he opened it and found

himself staring at a pair of boots. He looked up and saw that it was Stacklee. The black man said, "He's here, Calamaro."

"Shit," Nix said. He tried pulling the gun up but it was kicked away.

"Look at you. Guess you were right. Guess looking a nigger in the face is bad luck." Stacklee smiled. "Real bad luck."

Nix saw a blade in the black man's hand. He grabbed Stacklee's ankle and pulled, sending him down on his ass.

"Fucker," Stacklee said. He sliced Nix across the face and then kicked him in the head. After that, he thought it'd be over but the man attacked again, this time biting Stacklee on the ankle. "You biting me? Jesus Christ!"

Calamaro appeared behind Nix, grabbed a handful of hair, and sent a fist into the side of his head. The teeth held on, digging deeper into Stacklee's leg. Finally he pulled his gun and put it to the man's temple.

The pistol burped, sending a bullet into Nix's head. Chunks of brain bombarded the wall.

As Calamaro stood up, he heard a crack and felt a piercing and familiar pain on the side of his head. Another crack and the gun was knocked from his hand.

Chaps was standing in the doorway now, holding his whip. "Bring back memories?" he said.

Calamaro ducked and jumped into the room, sending his head into the bastard's stomach. Chaps doubled over but managed to wrap the whip around Calamaro's neck.

"Should've killed you when we had the chance," Chaps said. He pulled the whip tight while Calamaro pummeled him in the gut. In the doorway, Stacklee stood pointing his gun.

"Let him go, asshole," he said.

Chaps showed his goofy grin and said, "Okay." He let Calamaro go and then jumped backwards out the window, cracking his whip on the way down so it caught the bedpost. He landed safely on the ground below and then pulled his whip free.

Calamaro and Stacklee ran to the window. Chaps was running down the street, his dress blowing in the wind and his whip dragging behind him like a tail.

"Asshole got away," Stacklee said.

Calamaro nodded. "No, he didn't." He aimed his gun, resting it on his other arm. He squinted, watching Chaps run like a child until he made it to the blacksmith's place. Calamaro had him in his sights and then pulled the trigger.

Chaps went down hard, his chest leaking blood and his mouth still holding that silly grin. He hugged his whip to his chest and died.

Stacklee stared wide-eyed. He had never seen someone make such an accurate shot with a pistol especially one that burped. "Hey, that's a strange gun. Where's a man get something like that?"

"Found it on a farm," Calamaro said. "There was a whole bunch of them sticking out of the ground like flowers. Hundreds of them." He holstered the gun and then motioned for Stacklee to follow him out of the room. They needed to tell Kersey and the other people that it was safe to come back in now.

Calamaro said, "You can go back to Betty's."

"You sure you don't want to come with me? You might need a drink after this."

"I won't need a drink till the killing's done."

# CHAPTER THIRTY

Leonard woke up next to a tombstone.

A minute later Clayton sat up, sleepily hocking up phlegm and spitting it through the mouth-hole of his donkey mask.

Then Sergio awoke abruptly. He was always the last to get up, saying that he had nightmares that he couldn't escape from no matter how hard he tried. The nightmares were always the same. He was back in the prison camp. A confederate soldier is poking him with a thin, slimy sword. Sergio can feel himself bleeding but when he looks down, he only sees dust falling out of the wounds.

Then came the machine.

It was unlike any machine Sergio had ever seen and it always scared him how his brain could create something that didn't exist. It was made of green metal and red flesh. Its size never stayed the same. At first it was small enough to fit into the soldier's hands but as it crept closer to Sergio it grew to twice the size of a man. However, in most dreams it stayed small enough that the confederate soldier could hold it while it did things to Sergio that he could never bring himself to speak about.

The nightmares always ended the same way. A large figure smelling of alcohol and apples would come up behind him and say, "Are you ready for Captain Burroughs?" Sergio would feel a sharp pain in his scrotum and then he'd find himself crawling out of the prison camp and into the burning sun where his frowning father awaited him, shaking his head in disappointment.

Now fully awake, Sergio stood up. Leonard had the urge to ask him if he had the dream again but stopped himself. There was no use putting the man in a bad mood on the day they were going to pull their gold heist.

Leonard said, "You ready?"

"Yeah," Sergio said, running his hands through his dark hair. "I'm ready."

* * *

After he came back from getting his morning coffee, Mayor Douglas found another black envelope lying on top of his grey velvet couch.

There was no use in opening it. He knew the sort of picture that would be inside. Instead, he put it in his box of teeth along with the first photograph. He then rummaged through the box, looking for a tooth that would perhaps take his mind off the envelopes. He found it. It was a whore's tooth, cracked and yellow.

He popped it into his mouth and sucked on it. That always made him calmer. It was almost as if he was sucking the whore's life away. Later, he would sleep with it under his pillow and dream about the woman he got it from.

The memories started to get him aroused so he unbuttoned his pants and pulled them down.

"Jesus Christ!" he said. The red tattoos had spread and now covered not only his crotch and belly but his thighs as well. What was happening to him?

The new tattoos ruined his mood and Mayor Douglas decided not to jerk off to his teeth collection. Besides, a whole mess of trouble had blown through Screwhorse and he would ultimately be responsible for cleaning it up. Seems like running the town has been more hassle than it was worth. Perhaps he'd go to California and dabble in something that wouldn't give him such a headache. Maybe he'd invest in the Chinese slave trade. That'd make it easier for him to get pussy, that's for sure.

Mayor Douglas took a handful of whore-teeth from the box and tried using them to scrub the red tattoos off his body. When it didn't work, he threw the teeth across the room like dice.

He slammed his fists into his thighs, making them jiggle. "Fucking Italians..."

Then he heard several gunshots in the distance. What the fuck was happening now? The mayor pulled his pants up and headed out towards the jail. He'd have to beat some sense into that goddamn sheriff.

* * *

After Sheriff Doyle let Tom and Bluford out, he heard the shots coming from the hotel but didn't move an inch. He just knew it had something to do with that goddamned stranger who had some trouble with Nix Morrow. But Lyons said he had taken care of that, didn't he?

Doyle didn't feel like cleaning up another mess. It was bad enough there was someone going around killing whores. Too much shit happened in Screwhorse and he felt like he was getting too old to deal with it all. It wasn't that he didn't care. He never considered himself a bad man but sometimes it was easier just to go through the motions.

The door swung open.

"Jesus Christ, man, are you deaf or something?" Mayor Douglas said. "I even heard it from my house." His face was flushed and his belly looked even fatter than the last time Doyle saw it.

"Yeah, I heard."

Mayor Douglas slammed his knuckles down on the desk. "You get your ass over there and take care of things."

"You walked all the way down here just so you can tell

156

me how to do my job? With all due respect, mayor, I'd much rather sit here and let things fix themselves. I'm already busy having to deal with those killings at Betty's."

"Who gives a shit about some dirty whores?" Mayor Douglas said. "I don't need a goddamn shootout in the middle of my town. Next thing I know, they're sending in some government son of a bitch to investigate and then I'm out a job. And that means you'd be out of a job, too."

"Frankly, I wouldn't give a shit. Besides, none of this was my doing. Your man Lyons and his three assholes started this shit."

"I don't give a good goddamn who started it. You get the hell over there and take care of it or I'll have you tied to the railroad tracks. You ever been buggered by a Chinaman? It ain't pleasant. They know all sorts of tricks that'll make your ass bleed for days. Do you understand what I'm saying to you? You make any more excuses and I call my friend Shanghai Joe. Got it?"

Doyle said, "Sure do, mayor. I guess I'll go head over there, see if I could talk some sense into everyone."

"I was told that stranger was dead. Now I'm told by some whore that he's alive. If that stranger isn't dead yet, you better make sure he gets that way."

The sheriff picked up a shotgun and then stood in front of the mayor. "You keep talking, I'm not going to get a chance to do anything. You done?"

"Watch that smart mouth of yours or you'll be picking Chinese teeth out of your ass," he said, digging into his pocket and pulling out a whore's tooth. He held it up to show Doyle. "I'm going back to my house for a fuck. When I come back, all this shit better be finished, got it?"

"Yeah. I got it." Doyle walked out slowly. He figured he'd take his time looking into things. Who cared if the stranger was alive and taking care of business? Maybe he'd get rid of Lyons and his jackasses. That'd make his job as sheriff a hell of a lot easier.

# CHAPTER THIRTY-ONE

Sergio, Leonard, and Clayton walked up to the mayor's house. It was time to get to work.

They walked through a side door, one that was only used by the mayor's staff. As they entered, they heard the sound of heavy footsteps upstairs. Clayton and Leonard drew their guns but Sergio kept his holstered.

A skinny Chinaman walked out of the kitchen and stopped short when he saw the three men. His mouth opened wide to scream. Clayton ran up and punched him in the throat, sending him to the floor. A hard kick to the side of the head knocked the man out.

Sergio led the way upstairs to the mayor's office. They could hear more sounds now, not just footsteps. There was heavy breathing and squishy, thumping sounds. They stood in the hallway for a minute, waiting for the sounds to get more intense.

Then Sergio kicked open the door.

Mayor Douglas had his whore Ana bent over his desk. He was screwing her from behind while he was looking at a photograph he was holding up with his right hand. The screwing stopped. Clayton walked up to him and stuck a pistol in his tattoo-covered face.

"Get off the girl, you ugly motherfucker," Clayton said.

The mayor's face drooped in anger.

Clayton smiled and then pistol-whipped the fat man. "You really are an ugly cocksucker. Who gets tattoos on their face?"

"What the hell are you talking about?" the mayor said. He dropped the photograph and buttoned his pants.

"No, seriously. You should be the one wearing the mask," Clayton said. He turned to Leonard. "Don't you think so?"

"I don't think the mask would fit his fat fucking head, Clay." Leonard kept his gun aimed. He watched as Ana pulled away from the mayor. She said, "Thank you!" and then ran next to Sergio. As she did so, she looked at Mayor Douglas and gasped at the red tattoos that were now covering his face. They hadn't been there when they had started fucking.

"Oh my god!" she said. "What's wrong with you?"

Mayor Douglas said, "Shut up, you traitorous little whore!" He looked at Sergio. "Are you men mad? Have you any idea who I am? Do you?"

Sergio calmly stepped forward. "Oh, we do," he said. "You're the mayor. The question is: do you know who I am?"

The mayor squinted and shrugged. His eyes were ugly pinpoints beneath the tattoos. "No. Am I supposed to?"

Sergio took another step closer and drew his pistol. It was a huge gun, one that dwarfed both Leonard's and Clayton's. It was carved out of ivory and had intricate red designs on the barrel. He pointed it at the mayor's head. "My name is Sergio," he said. "Sergio Cardinale."

# CHAPTER THIRTY-TWO

Bluford Barnes didn't know what the hell to do.

There was no way the sheriff would believe him. Tom Duma had an alibi and a stranger from out of town wasn't going to be able to prove anything different. Thinking about Lily and how she was gutted, Bluford decided he was going to take care of things himself.

The only problem was that he didn't have a weapon. He did know how to throw a punch or two, one of the few things he had learned from his pugilist brother. If it came down to it, maybe he could knock Tom Duma out and find some proof that he was behind the killings.

But who was he kidding? He was a card cheat and nothing more.

Doubt overcame Bluford. How could he confront a murderer? He had always lived his life in the proverbial shadows, deceiving and drawing as little attention to himself as possible. The rule was to never get involved in any serious matter that went on in a town and that included multiple murders.

But this was different. He couldn't help shake the feeling that if he hadn't taken Lily up to her room, she'd still be alive. There was a part of him that felt responsible even though he wasn't the one who actually committed the gruesome crime.

So Bluford let his conscience take over. He ran toward the General Store and went around the side, peeking in the windows. Through the smudged glass he saw Tom Duma pointing his finger in his wife's face and screaming. "It was my secret! Mine!"

Bluford watched as Tom then wrapped his hands around his wife's throat, squeezing hard, still yelling.

His wife was hysterical. "I did it for you! I did it so they'd let you out!" She brought up her own hands and Bluford saw that she was wearing black leather gloves, slick with blood.

Tom Duma grabbed one of the gloves off his wife's hand and stuck it into her mouth. Her eyes widened as she gagged but she made no move to fight back against her husband.

Bluford pulled away from the window, ran to the back door and went inside. He lunged at Tom Duma, hoping to knock him out with a few punches.

Mrs. Duma spat out the glove and screamed, "Don't you dare touch my husband!"

Tom took three hits to the face before running out of the house, leaving his wife hysterically crying and cursing at Bluford. She jumped on him, knocking him down, and then ran up the stairs.

Bluford stood up and quickly made the choice to follow Mrs. Duma and not her husband. He wasn't sure if it was his cowardice or chivalry that was behind that decision but he made it anyway. When he reached the top of the stairs, he saw her at the end of the hallway. She was no longer crying. She was filled with calm anger.

She said, "You know, don't you?"

"That you killed the girls?"

Mrs. Duma smiled. "Not all of them."

Seeing the woman's crazed expression made Bluford realize that he had made the wrong decision in following her. There was something extremely dangerous about the woman. Her eyes were filled with rage and death.

"Why?" he said. "Why kill anyone?"

"I couldn't let the sheriff lock Tom up."

"So it was true? Your husband killed Lily?"

"Yeah, so what business of it is yours? He had to kill her. There's a lot about Tom no one knows."

Bluford was both confused and terrified. Why the hell would she be confessing to all of this? There were only two possibilities. Either she was planning to give herself up or she was planning to kill him. If she was capable of killing two innocent girls then would she probably wouldn't hesitate in killing him now that he knew her secret.

Despite his terror, he made a grab for Mrs. Duma but was surprised to find that she was both strong and fast. She knocked him down and ran into a bedroom. He followed, her musky perfume invading his nostrils. It reminded him of seawater and menstrual blood.

The bedroom was full of broken dolls, most with their eyes poked out and their heads torn from their bodies. Several of them were covered in black lace and some were made of glass. There were newspapers scattered on the floor along with a camera and a pile of black envelopes.

Mrs. Duma grabbed a glass doll from the floor and held it up. "Whores!" She smashed it against the wall and then picked up another one. "Whores, all of them!"

Bluford decided to play along since the woman was in such a frenzied and unpredictable state. "Yeah, I know. They're whores." He took a step closer but she held her black-gloved hand out.

"Don't get any closer!" she said. "Or I'll do to you what I did to those dirty little cunts!"

"Relax, Mrs. Duma, just relax."

"Don't tell me to relax, you little cocksucker. You prance into town without a second thought about the people in it. You don't think about the mayor and his killers. You don't think about the sickness that runs through here." She held a glass doll up above her head. "This town's a hell! Do you hear me? A hell!"

# CHAPTER THIRTY-THREE

William Lyons wiped his mouth. He patted his wife's hand and said, "That was a wonderful meal, love. Really hit the spot."

Catherine blushed and nodded. "I'm glad you liked it."

"Boys, did you thank your mother for making such a delicious meal?"

The two young children at the table smiled and shouted, "Thank you, ma!" and then ran off to play.

"Those little ones sure are cute, Cath," William said. "I still can't believe I had a part in making them."

"Yes, they're our little angels." Catherine was starting to clean the dishes when there was a knock on the door. "You expecting company, William?"

"No, I'm not," he said, standing up. "Why don't you take the boys into the sewing room?"

Catherine put her hands to her chest. "Oh my, what's happening, William?"

"Probably nothing but take them nonetheless."

Before either of them could move, both of the boys ran to the front door and opened it. Their father yelled. "Get your asses back here!"

One of the boys said, "There's no one here. Someone just left a toy."

William walked over to the door, grabbing his pistol on the way over. He pushed his boys towards their mother and watched them run into the sewing room.

The kids were only half right. Yes, there was no one there but the hell if someone had left a toy. It wasn't a toy at all.

It was a wooden donkey.

William put a hand on the door to slam it shut when the mouth of the donkey opened up with a fiery blast. He was blown back by the small explosion, landing on the table that he had built for Catherine for their anniversary.

Then he saw that bastard standing in the doorway, the bastard he left in the desert to die.

Calamaro smiled. "We were never properly introduced. William Lyons, is it?"

"You little cocksucker."

"Let's not get ahead of ourselves." Calamaro winked.

William lifted his pistol and pulled the trigger hard, sending a bullet in Calamaro's direction but missing by a good six inches. That's when William heard the burp. At first he thought it came from him since, after all, he did just eat. Then he realized that it came from the doorway. Did the stranger actually have the nerve to belch? William heard it again and he saw that it hadn't come from the stranger's mouth but from his gun.

That's when he felt the pain of a bullet in each of his kneecaps. William lifted his pistol but didn't aim it. It was shot out of his hand with another burping bullet.

"Fuck you," he said. He started crawling to the cellar door. It wasn't much of a cellar, just a small area that he had dug out himself. It looked like the stranger wasn't going to stop him. The stupid bastard had no idea what he kept down there. He held the doorknob to the cellar and said, "Hey asshole, you ever heard of syphilis?"

Calamaro said, "Afraid not."

Lyons coughed and when he did, his wounds pumped more blood onto the floor.

"It's a disease. You get it from whores. My younger brother, he's a doctor, lives in London, he told me all about it and I've never been able to get it out of my head, you know?

Well, this disease does a lot to a man's mind, makes them crazy enough to eat the devil with horns on."

"There a point to this story?" Calamaro said. He held his gun up, eager to hear it burp again.

"The point is that I've always been fascinated with how a man can go and screw some whore with a dirty cunny, have a few minutes of pleasure not knowing they're leaving with a disease that'll rot his brain out. Tell me that doesn't fascinate you."

Calamaro pointed his gun at William Lyons' head. "I imagine you're talking for a reason, trying to get my guard down or something. Sorry to disappoint you but it's not going to work."

"No, I'm just trying to prepare you for what's coming." William Lyons turned the knob, opened the door, and whistled.

Out of the darkness of the basement came a din of footsteps and groans. Then a rush of pale, naked bodies as more than two dozen syphilitic men ran out, almost trampling Lyons as he rolled out of the way. The men ran forward, stumbling like a drunken hoard.

Calamaro lifted his gun to shoot but they were coming too fast. He backed out of the house and almost tripped down the stairs. The mob of sick men came shuffling out, pushing aside the wooden donkey. A few of them tried exiting at the same time and got stuck in the doorway.

Kimama came running from around the side of the house. He saw the hesitation in Calamaro. Who wanted to shoot at a group of men who were obviously sick and probably dying? The Indian shouted. "Shoot, Calamaro! If you want to live, shoot!"

The group of syphilitics looked so pathetic and crazed Calamaro wasn't sure he wanted to just shoot them all down. But as they came out of the doorway, their mouths drooling foam, rushing to him with their arms outstretched, he decided he had no choice.

He emptied his gun into the mass of naked flesh.

The ones he hit yelped and spun around but continued forward as if not realizing they were shot. He hit another one of them in the chest, making a hole that exposed a rotted ribcage.

Kimama was swinging his shovel like an axe through the crowd of diseased men. Blood splattered, flesh flew off in flakes that danced in the desert wind, and teeth fell to the ground like seeds. When he stopped swinging, Kimama had killed five of the syphilitics. Some of the ones he didn't kill ran away towards the center of town as if realizing that the Indian was not one to be reckoned with.

Calamaro held his ground, punching and kicking while reloading his gun and shooting at the remaining men who looked more confused than dangerous. The crazed men kept charging despite being shot several times. Calamaro wondered how screwing a whore could turn a man into that. They were barely human beings.

One of the men sat down on the ground and looked up at Calamaro. He stuck his fingers into his mouth, plucked out a tooth and said, "You want to know what William does to us? He comes down to the cellar and sticks his fist in us because he can't get his pecker hard enough to screw his wife." He looked at Calamaro and pointed to the men that Kimama had killed. "You can clean up the mess, but don't touch their coffins. You may have to drag them across the desert."

A bullet ripped through the man's head, shattering it into a cloud of confetti made of brain, skull, and blood. William Lyons stood in the doorway on his wounded legs. He smiled and pointed the gun at Calamaro. "That fucker never could keep his mouth shut."

The surviving syphilitics saw what had happened so they quickly dispersed, giving up on their attack.

Calamaro said, "You'd shoot a sick man who wasn't even looking at you?"

"Don't act like a saint, Calamaro. Why'd you come

to this town? Whores? Gold? Who the hell do you think you are? This is my fucking town."

Calamaro nodded. "Your town? That changed once you buried me up to my neck. You'd do the same you were in my position, don't you think?"

"I don't really give a shit."

"Well, then," Calamaro said. He dropped to the ground and rolled towards Sartana, sending a hard kick to the wooden donkey's backside. Another blast of flames and shrapnel erupted out of its mouth and engulfed William Lyons, blowing him back into his house.

He trembled and bled profusely on the floor.

Calamaro and Kimama stood over William. It was amazing that the man was still alive.

"You have anything to say?" Calamaro kicked him in the leg.

William Lyons looked up at the ceiling. "Look what you've done. My sons won't have a father and that's all because of you. When they grow up, I imagine they'll realize what happened and get angry enough to hunt you down and kill you. Especially Ringo. That boy has a temper. He'll be coming for you sure enough." He leaned his head back. "You know, Calamaro, you'll see me in Hell and when we're there, I'm going to skin you alive." He coughed up blood and started shivering. "It's cold in here. Close the door."

Calamaro humored the man and closed it.

Lyons continued. "Put me in the cellar. Let me die in peace, will you?"

Calamaro thought about how it might be the honorable thing to do but then he remembered being buried up to his neck in the desert. He remembered his face being slashed and being made to eat his own flesh. Then he remembered the murder of his wife and daughter. He remembered walking in on the killers and seeing that they all looked like William Lyons.

Calamaro said, "William, I just can't do that. You understand?"

"I understand you're a fucking cocksucker."

Calamaro held his weapon out, pointed it at William's heart, and pulled the trigger.

The pistol burped and then William Lyons was dead.

Kimama was silent, still holding his shovel that was now covered in brains, hair, and scalp-flesh. He was glad Lyons was dead but knew that he had to do one last thing to make sure the man's bad spirit didn't live on. He raised his shovel and rammed the sharp end into William's skull.

It cracked open like an egg. A mess of brains and blood oozed out along with dozens of tiny two-tailed scorpions. They crawled out in all directions as if happy to be freed from their prison. He left his shovel embedded in the floor in between the two halves of William's head.

"Guess I'll go to Betty's and say my goodbyes," Calamaro said.

Kimama smiled. "You do that. I cannot join you, though. I'm going back into the desert. I have done enough here."

"Thank you."

"You are welcome, Calamaro."

With that, the two men parted ways.

Calamaro leaned against the house, relieved that the bulk of the fighting was over. He was about to holster his gun when he heard the sounds of yelling. It was the Indians.

They were attacking the town.

* * *

"Oh my god," Mayor Douglas said. The man named Sergio Cardinale was standing in front of him, pointing a gun and looking like a vicious but patient dog ready to attack. But he wouldn't. He probably wanted to have a little fun before he got his revenge. "You're Belladonna's husband?"

Sergio shook his head. "Brother."

The mayor nodded slowly and looked at the floor. He thought he could probably reach the gun he kept under his desk. If only he could play the part of the slow and helpless fat man well enough. He put his hands out in front of him. "Oh god, please don't kill me. Oh my god, please, forgive me. Forgive me!"

"God may forgive bastards like you," Sergio said. "But I don't."

Mayor Douglas made his move. He grabbed the gun underneath his desk and pointed it at Sergio.

Leonard and Clayton had their weapons aimed, ready to shoot if Sergio gave the word. Three guns against one were pretty good odds but they didn't want to lose Sergio.

The mayor said, "You want revenge, that it? So your whore of a sister is dead and now you think killing me is going to satisfy you. You think it'll get rid of the guilt you have for not being there to protect her? Killing me isn't going to bring her back."

"Not bring her back," Sergio said. "Just make it so you don't get the chance to enjoy yourself anymore."

The mayor looked at Ana. "And this little Mexican cunt is helping you, huh? This little two-faced bitch?"

Sergio said, "You don't like women much, do you?"

Mayor Douglas laughed. "And you do? Don't let this whore fool you. Before I took her as my own personal cunt, she was the mistress of General Santo Leche. Ever hear of him? He was a general down in Mexico during the Battle of Puebla. You know what happened to him after his victory against those French bastards? This bitch here killed him in his sleep. Slit his throat like a pig. That's why I never fall asleep unless I know the doors are locked. This little Mexican cunt who was so nice in helping you? She'd kill you for a cigarette."

Sergio knew the man was right. Even though she was the one who sent him the message that Mayor Douglas had his parents killed and his sister kidnapped, Ana didn't seem like someone who could be trusted. She was also the one who clued him in on the gold which probably meant she had an interest in it, too.

Without warning, Mayor Douglas turned the gun on Ana and sent a bullet through her right breast. She fell backward and convulsed.

Sergio pulled the trigger and let a shot go off right on the side of the mayor's head, startling the man.

Ana whispered, "Bastard."

"Shut up, whore," Mayor Douglas said.

"You pull that trigger again and I'll make sure it takes you weeks to die," Sergio said.

The fat man scoffed. "You boys aren't stupid enough to kill a mayor."

Clayton stepped forward. "I'm going to rough him up a bit."

"No," Sergio said. "He's going to unlock his vault and give us the gold. Then I'm going to kill him. Deep down he knows it. Just won't admit it to himself."

"Maybe I won't leave this house alive," Mayor Douglas said. "But I'm taking you with me."

Sergio saw his opportunity, grabbed the mayor's weapon, and then punched him in the gut, sending the fat man to the ground.

Leonard said, "Mayor. It'll be best if you just let us have that gold."

Mayor Douglas crawled to the wall behind his desk and pushed a button. A part of the wall opened up, revealing the door to his vault. He got to his knees to reach the combination lock.

As soon as Sergio heard the click that let him know the vault was unlocked, he put his gun to the mayor's head.

"I'm just letting you know I'm not giving you the luxury of saying any last words."

He pulled the trigger. Brains and skull splattered the door to the vault.

Clayton laughed, ran forward, and pulled the vault door open.

"Holy shit," he said.

Leonard stepped forward. "What the hell?"

Sergio looked inside. "Christ Almighty."

There was no gold in the vault, not one piece. It wasn't filled with currency of any kind.

It was filled with corpses.

For the first time in weeks, Clayton took the donkey mask off. He stared in at the bodies. "So where in the hell is all that gold?"

Before either of the other men could respond, they heard shouting from down the street. They looked out the window and saw Indians riding into town.

Leonard said, "Looks like Hell just rode into Screwhorse. Let's get out of here."

* * *

"Okay, just calm yourself down." Bluford had never struck a woman and would have never thought he would contemplate it. After meeting Mrs. Duma, however, he was getting ready to jump forward and punch the bitch in the jaw. Before he could do so, she grabbed a razor out of her dress pocket and lunged forward with it, cutting Bluford in the neck.

"Whores!" she screamed, shaking the glass doll that was in her other hand. Her face was an inch from Bluford's. "These whores are ruining everything, spreading their diseases, turning men into monsters! Look at what they did to my brother, making him so sick that William Lyons locked him up in his cellar. He's barely a man anymore!"

Bluford had no idea what she was talking about but figured that any killer was going to come up with a variety of creative excuses for their crimes.

So he slapped her.

"Cocksucker!" she screamed and then slammed the glass doll into his nose. He fell back, pulling her on top of him. As they struggled, the sound of hoof beats and screams came through the window. They both got to their knees and looked outside.

Bluford couldn't believe what he was seeing. "Holy shit."

Mrs. Duma's mouth opened in shock. "Indians."

# CHAPTER THIRTY-FOUR

Sergio said, "What the hell is going on?"

"I don't know," Leonard said. "But I know it's nothing we should stick around for."

Clayton pulled the mask back over his face. "Fucking redskins."

They ran out of the room and left the mayor's house.

On the other side of town, the Indians were screaming loudly, creating a morbid chorus in a tongue that none of the three men understood.

"That's the strangest fucking language I've ever heard," Clayton said. "It sounds like they're burping or something."

They were running so quickly that they neglected to see a group of Indian women, wrapped in blankets, slowly approaching them.

"Jesus Christ," Clayton said, pointing at the women. "Squaws."

Sergio pulled his weapon. "Stop."

The women either didn't understand or didn't care. They kept walking.

Clayton stepped forward, pulling his weapon and pointing it at one of the women. "You heard the man, you fucking redskin cunts. Stop."

They didn't stop.

As they got closer, Clayton saw their faces. Each was covered with green blotches.

"What the fuck's going on?" he said. "Didn't you hear me? Stop!"

The women dropped their blankets, revealing their nakedness.

Clayton's jaw dropped at the sight of their heavy, sagging breasts. He was surprised that in a situation like this, he was still able to be stunned by the sight of female flesh. In his aroused trance, he didn't see one of the women hold a blade up over her shoulder, ready to throw it directly into his chest.

Sergio pulled his gun, getting three shots off, and all three women went down.

"Fucking pay attention, Clay," he said. "Leonard and I don't have time to bury your ass."

"Shit," Clayton said. "Those tits were just so….."

"Keep it together or you're likely to get your dick shot off."

They managed to slip out of town before the bulk of the Indians made it to the mayor's house.

"Shit, we should've brought some water with us," Clayton said.

"Yeah, that would've probably been a good idea," Leonard said, realizing just how dry his mouth was. Then he looked at Sergio and said, "You should've told us why you wanted to come here. We wouldn't have had a problem with it."

Clayton said, "Yeah, we would've understood."

Sergio nodded. "I figured if I told you it was about my sister, you wouldn't want to risk your asses for it. It was my problem, not yours."

"It's okay," Clayton said. "I may be a bastard but I have family, too. If someone did something to my sister, well…."

Leonard gave him a look that told him to shut the hell up.

"I'm just sorry there wasn't any gold to make this worth your while," Sergio said.

"Yeah," Clayton said. "Where the hell is all that gold?"

# CHAPTER THIRTY-FIVE

Calamaro dragged Sartana down the street, staring at the carnage that was unfolding before his eyes. He had just got done killing William Lyons and thought that he was done with death. He was wrong.

The violence was erupting in front of him. Some of the townspeople were being pulled into the street and disemboweled. Others were being beaten with sticks made of green bone. As some of the Indians rode closer to Calamaro, he readied himself for action. Dropping Sartana's reins, he pulled his gun out and quickly got several shots off, hitting a group of Indians. Each went down with a shattered skull.

Calamaro knew that he wouldn't be able to survive with only his gun so he grabbed a hatchet from one of the corpses. The weapon was extremely lightweight and strong. It was made of a pink, spongy material. He swung it a few times and listened to it whistle through the air. It sounded like a scream.

With one hand he dragged Sartana and with the other, he hacked away at whatever Indian dared cross his path. The pink sponge-hatchet worked wonders, splitting skulls open and severing limbs with ease. Then Calamaro saw a large group of Indians running toward him.

He put Sartana's reins down and then pushed a button on the underside of the wooden donkey. There were a few clicks and then a fuse appeared from the donkey's nostrils.

Calamaro took a match from his pocket, lit it, and put it up to the fuse. "Sorry, Sartana, old friend. This is where we part ways."

Calamaro lit the fuse.

Then he ran like hell.

The group of Indians ran to the donkey, thinking that it was just something else to destroy. Calamaro watched them raise their weapons to it.

The wooden donkey exploded, sending flaming women's shoes everywhere. High heels and razors were sticking out of the Indians who were foolish enough to have approached Sartana. They screamed in agony, trying to pull the shoes from their flesh.

Calamaro turned to look at the brothel down the road. There were no Indians attacking it yet but several of the syphilitic men were at the door as if wanting to spread their disease to the whores who had given it to them.

He bolted down the street, dodging corpses and raging Indians who tried striking him with their bizarre weaponry. Through the bloodshed, he made it to the front of the brothel.

Just as he was pointing his gun to fend off the syphilitics, Calamaro heard voices from behind him yelling for help. He turned and saw the sheriff and another man surrounded by Indians. There was no good reason why he should help them. Many men in his position would simply turn their backs and get to safety. But Calamaro couldn't turn his back on them, even though he wanted nothing else but to lie down and sleep for days.

Now the syphilitics were banging on the brothel door, flakes of skin falling to the ground with each fist-thrust. Then more yells for help from the two men.

Calamaro froze.

For once in his life, he was paralyzed by indecision.

* * *

Bluford tried holding Mrs. Duma back but her anger and insanity overpowered him. Still carrying her glass doll, she ran downstairs and out the back door, right into the clutches of an Indian.

"You goddamn heathen!" she screamed. "You cocksucking redskin! You...."

Her tirade was cut short by the Indian's fist as it slammed into her nose. She dropped to the ground. The Indian grabbed Mrs. Duma's glass doll from her hand and shoved it into her mouth.

She gagged on the doll, drool rising up out of her mouth and onto her cheeks. The Indian shoved it in deeper. Mrs. Duma gagged again, sounding like an out-of-breath duck.

Soon the glass doll was so far down Mrs. Duma's throat, the Indian was able to close her mouth.

After she choked to death, Mrs. Duma's corpse was used as a latrine by the Indian who then invited a few of his fellow invaders to do the same. When Bluford snuck down the stairs and looked out the window, all he saw was a woman's body covered in lumps of green and pink shit.

Not wanting to succumb to a similar fate, Bluford ran out the other door. He was prepared to use all of his strength to at least put up a good fight. There was no way he was dying like an animal at the hands of those savages.

As he went out the front door, Bluford ran right into Sheriff Doyle.

"Jesus Christ!" the sheriff said. "Come on!" He grabbed Bluford and guided him into the street. "We have to get some horses and get the fuck out of here."

Just as soon as it seemed like they'd have a clear path to a pair of horses in front of the brothel, a group of Indians surrounded them.

"What now?" Bluford said, watching as more Indians

were now dismembering the pair of horses.

"I don't know," Sheriff Doyle said. "I don't fucking know."

* * *

When the Indians started to attack, Betty thought that God himself had sent the Devil and his demons into Screwhorse to pass judgment on its wickedness.

It wasn't that she necessarily believed in any of those bible stories but just the sight of those redskins put fear into her heart. They weren't like any other Indians she had ever seen. Their bodies contorted in grotesque ways, many of them crawling along the street like scorpions. The weapons they held were strange and seemed to be made from a combination of metal, bone, and flesh.

After the initial shock and screaming, the only ones left in the bar were Betty, Stacklee, and Black Boned Keith. Betty told the men to help her move tables and chairs in front of the doors. They moved quickly, making sure to block every possible entrance. Luckily none of the Indians were approaching them.

Stacklee said, "Looks like they aren't attacking the brothel."

"Maybe we'll get lucky and they'll forget about us," Black Boned Keith said.

Betty pointed across the street. "Look at what they're doing to Doctor West."

Several Indians had a hold of the doctor and were impaling him with a long green spear.

Stacklee said, "Oh my god."

Betty grabbed his shoulder. "What?"

"The Brady sisters." He pointed down the street where a group of nude Indian men were carrying Goldie and Blanche Brady over their shoulders. The women looked unharmed.

Betty started to cry. It was one thing seeing her fellow townspeople being slaughtered but to see two of her own girls being taken away by those redskins was another. That broke her heart.

Black Boned Keith said, "You know they aren't going to kill those girls. Not yet, anyway. Going to take them back to their camp, make them their squaws."

Stacklee had to use all his energy not to punch the man in the mouth. "Shut up, Keith."

"I'm just saying. Maybe they're the lucky ones." Keith walked away and poured himself a drink at the bar.

Both Stacklee and Betty grabbed guns, waiting by the door in case any of the Indians decided to attack. None of them did.

Instead, a group of pale men approached the brothel doors. Their skin was falling off, ribs were peeking out of their chests, and their faces were covered in dust and spittle.

"Let us in!" they cried. "We're paying customers!" One of the syphilitics pulled his own nipple off, holding it up as if it were a coin.

"Shoot the fuckers, Stack," Keith said.

"That'd be pretty stupid, shooting them through the windows. Don't you think?"

Stacklee watched closely to see just what those sick men could be capable of doing. They didn't look strong enough to get inside so maybe the best thing to do would be to wait them out.

Betty shouted, "Calamaro!" She pointed down the street.

"I'm going out there," Stacklee said.

Betty grabbed his arm. "Don't you dare! I don't need two good men dying today."

They watched as Calamaro pulled his wooden donkey and then stopped. He fiddled with it and then struck a match.

"What's he doing?" Betty said.

"I imagine something's going to blow up." Stacklee shook his head. "Blow some Indians to hell."

Calamaro jumped away from the donkey and then it exploded, sending debris everywhere, killing several Indians. Screams for help came from across the street. Bluford Barnes and Sheriff Doyle were surrounded by Indians.

Betty watched now as Calamaro approached the brothel. The syphilitic men at the door were getting more excited, banging their heads until hair and scalp-flesh fell off.

"Stacklee, help me get him in," she said.

"We can't do it now unless we want those other bastards coming in with him." Stacklee pointed at Calamaro. "And anyway, it looks like he's changing his mind."

Calamaro was frozen in place, one hand holding the pink hatchet and the other holding his gun.

Betty said, "We have to do something."

"Yeah," Stacklee said. "But what?"

\* \* \*

Calamaro stood in the midst of bloodshed.

He could easily save himself and fight his way to the brothel but that wouldn't be a choice he'd be proud of making. So he tightened his grip on the hatchet and went into the street, hacking away at one Indian after another until he got to Sheriff Doyle and Bluford.

"I ran out of bullets," Doyle said.

Calamaro nodded. He didn't need an explanation as to why the man couldn't defend himself against the redskins. He handed the hatchet to Doyle. "Here."

The three men walked the short but bloody trail back to the brothel.

Bluford stood between the sheriff and Calamaro while they chopped and shot their way through the crowd of attackers.

180

Limbs were hacked off, faces were blown to pieces, and screams of agony echoed through the street.

It was unnatural to Bluford to see such violence first-hand. Calamaro, the man with the disfigured face and the burping gun was shooting Indians in the head so rapidly that the brains that splattered out of the redskin skulls looked like fast falling snow. When his bullets ran out, Calamaro had no time to reload so he used the butt of his gun to break noses and jaws.

The Indians did their best to try to kill them with their weird weapons. One in particular seemed intent on killing Doyle but the sheriff kept hacking away as if in a trance. Bluford couldn't believe the bloodlust in his eyes. The pink hatchet itself glowed with iridescent blood and seemed to swell with each successful act of violence against Indian flesh.

Finally, the trio made it to the brothel steps only to be met with the syphilitics. The diseased men turned their attention to Bluford, the only unarmed man in the group. They quickly shuffled toward him.

Though Sheriff Doyle had no reason to protect Bluford, he jumped into action. It was still his town. It was bad enough he hadn't been able to defend all the rest of the townspeople who were being dragged from their houses and gruesomely killed in the street.

With his pink hatchet in hand, Doyle struck at the syphilitics. He hit one of the men in the neck, nearly decapitating him. Blood gushed out of the wound and onto Doyle. He finished by sending the hatchet into the man's face.

Another one leaped forward and grabbed Bluford but the hatchet came down in between his sunken eyes. Brains spilled out, covering the syphilitic's face in grey fungi.

"Get in the fucking brothel. Now!" Doyle screamed, pushing Bluford in that direction. Behind him, Calamaro was still using his gun to finish off the attackers.

All three men approached the brothel door and inside, Betty and Stacklee were moving the tables out of the way so they could be let in. Calamaro held a large Indian at bay and said, "You two get inside!"

Sheriff Doyle and Bluford ran up the steps and into the brothel.

Calamaro was hit in the chest by the Indian's weapon, a giant red claw with pink teeth sticking out of it. The wound wasn't deep and he was able to strike back at the redskin. One more hit caused the Indian to fall backward and Calamaro ran into the brothel.

\* \* \*

Sergio stopped walking. He crouched down next to a cactus and said, "I wish we had some water."

Leonard nodded. "Some food, too. I'm hungry as hell."

From behind them, there was the sound of flames. Clayton said, "Look."

Sergio and Leonard saw the town of Screwhorse in the distance. The Indians had hoisted someone up onto the roof of the mayor's house and then set that person on fire.

"You think that's a warning? A sign telling people not to mess with redskins?" Clayton said.

"No," Sergio said. "I think it's a sign of victory."

Leonard said, "You think we should've stayed? Helped some people get out?"

"Hell no. They're not kin to us. We don't owe them anything," Clayton said. "And anyway, we do that, we'd probably not get out alive. Right, Sergio?"

Sergio didn't reply. The sight of the burning corpse brought back memories of the prison camp. He had buried that part of his life as much as possible but after his time in Screwhorse, it was all coming back to him.

He remembered the confederate officer who made his life hell. There hadn't been a day or even an hour that

Captain Clark Burroughs didn't do something to humiliate or torture Sergio. But still, Burroughs could never make Sergio Cardinale cry or beg for mercy and maybe that's why the torture continued until the very end.

The captain was the one that told Sergio about the message he had received from a Mexican woman named Ana. Sergio's parents had been killed and his sister Belladonna abducted. She was being held by the mayor of a desert town called Screwhorse. Captain Burroughs delighted in this information and talked about it for hours in front of Sergio, waiting for the prisoner to crack.

"Your whore of a sister must be sucking that mayor's dick right about now. Sucking his dick while her brother is rotting away here in a goddamn prison camp. She must be so proud," the captain had said on the last day Sergio was held captive.

Sergio had nodded slowly, sweat sliding down his face. He couldn't think of anything to say that would have wounded the captain. So instead, he made his move and pulled out the makeshift knife he had been preparing and shoved it into Clark's neck.

So as he watched the Indian's slaughter of Screwhorse from afar, Sergio thought about how he slipped into the captain's uniform and started to shoot and slash his way out of the camp. His escape route was a bloody path filled with the half-eaten flesh and bleached bones of his fellow Union soldiers.

He started feeling feverish but it wasn't from the heat. His mouth became like cotton and the veins in his neck throbbed with uncertain anger.

Once again Sergio looked at the flaming corpse. "Yeah," he said. "We really should've brought some water with us."

\* \* \*

Stacklee and Sheriff Doyle slammed the door behind Calamaro and then pushed the tables in front of it.

"This shit's only going to get worse," Sheriff Doyle said. He looked at Calamaro and couldn't help but look at the wounds on the man's face instead of his eyes. It took all of his self-control not to show disgust. "Thanks for getting us out of that mess. I misjudged you."

Calamaro nodded and then turned to Betty, practically falling into her arms. His wounds were leaking blood and drool, soaking her dress.

"Honey...oh, honey," she said, holding him in her arms.

Sheriff Doyle said, "Okay, we have to come up with a plan and fast. Those fucking bastards outside are going to eventually want in here and I don't know if we can defend against more than a few of those redskins at once."

Black Boned Keith walked over from the bar. "I'll tell you what I'm going to do. I'm going to leave this fucking town out the back. Our best chance is to leave now."

"That's a bad idea, if you ask me," Stacklee said. "I think we should wait until we know what their plan is."

"Fuck that. We wait, we're going to end up trapped in here," Keith said. "And I for one don't want to be eaten by those fucking savages. I'm taking my cattle and getting the hell out of Screwhorse."

Stacklee laughed. "Are you kidding me? You think you're getting out of here with your herd?"

"Damn right." Keith walked toward the back door. "Anyone else want to come with me, come on."

Everyone stayed put, not trusting that Black Boned Keith's idea was the best. But one voice interrupted the stillness.

"I'll go with you!" Mary ran downstairs. "I'm not going to die here. I'm not going to be a whore killed by Indians."

"Why the hell didn't you leave before like I told you to?" Betty said.

"Timothy Horn didn't want me to."

"So where is that bastard?"

"Passed out drunk on the floor."

Betty rolled her eyes. "Guess we should wake him up."

"No!" Mary said.

All eyes were on her.

Sheriff Doyle said, "Why the hell not?"

"Because," Mary said. She turned her back on the group. "Because he's dead."

Stacklee moved to comfort her but Doyle put his arm out and said, "What happened, Mary?"

"He got rough with me."

"And?"

"I killed him."

Sheriff Doyle shook his head. "How?"

"I stepped on his throat while he was sleeping."

Betty let out a cry. It wasn't that she gave a shit about Timothy Horn but to hear that one of her own girls had murdered a man in his sleep was enough to make anyone upset.

"Mary, please answer this carefully," Sheriff Doyle said. "Do you know anything about the girls that were killed here?"

"No!" Mary said. "Of course not!"

"Did Timothy?"

"I don't know. I mean, he didn't say anything about it."

Bluford said, "I know who did it."

"What're you talking about?" Doyle said. "Who did it?"

"Tom Duma and his wife."

"Shit, didn't we clear this up?"

Bluford explained about the previous night, the shadowy figure in the coat and hat, and the confrontation with the Dumas. Everyone seemed surprised that those two could've

185

been capable of such atrocities but in the circumstances, they didn't seem to be incapacitated by the news.

Doyle looked over his shoulder. He saw the Indians outside dragging Kersey through the street. It was a horrible sight, seeing the man defenseless against those savages. And he, the sheriff, couldn't do anything about it.

"Okay, here's what we're going to do. We'll wait. Savages or not, they probably have some sort of plan. Probably a plan that they learned from fighting the goddamn U.S. Army all these years. Soon as we learn what they're doing, we take off, go up to Keoma. Everybody agree?"

Black Boned Keith said, "No, you know damn well I don't agree. And Mary can come with me if she wants. What about June? She's still here, right?"

"She's sick, probably still sleeping," Stacklee said. "I'll go get her."

Sheriff Doyle turned to Calamaro. "What do you think, stranger? You waiting for us or going with that son of a bitch?"

Calamaro shook his head. "I'm staying. At least for a while."

"Okay, then, Keith," Doyle said. "You and Mary go but if you try to come back, we're not going to let you in if there's a hoard of Indians following you. Got it?"

"Yeah, sheriff. Sure," Keith said. He took Mary by the arm and walked her out the back door.

"There goes two dead idiots," Sheriff Doyle said.

"So what does that make us?" Betty said, listening to the growing noise of violence outside.

* * *

Stacklee knocked on the door. "June? You feeling any better?"

There was no answer.

186

He knocked again and then walked in. What he saw made him drop to his knees and vomit.

In the middle of the room, June was naked on the floor. Her breasts were bubbling, the nipples ejaculating thin pink strands of hair. Red tattoos covered the rest of her flesh.

"Oh my god," Stacklee said. He crawled toward June but knew that despite the movement of her body, she wasn't alive, at least not like she was before. He looked into her eyes and saw only death.

The hair that squeezed out of her nipples was now shooting onto Stacklee. He shoved it aside and shivered when he did so. Quickly, he left the room and walked down the stairs, wondering how Betty would take the news. She had already lost three girls to murder, two more to the Indians, and one just committed a murder herself.

"Betty," he said. "June's dead."

"Oh my god, I'm in hell." Betty said. "This is hell." She let go of Calamaro and walked over to the bar.

Sheriff Doyle took Stacklee aside. "What happened to her? June, I mean."

"I don't know. Some strange shit's going on. Her body's all….messed up."

"Cut up like the others?"

"I don't think so," Stacklee said. His eyes filled up with tears. "I don't know what happened to her but I know she didn't deserve it."

"I know." Sheriff Doyle turned to Calamaro. "You're pretty quiet."

Calamaro attempted a smile but his wounds made it appear as if he was scowling. "You want me to give a speech?" he said.

Doyle chuckled. "No, guess not."

"Look," Stacklee said, pointing outside. Black Boned Keith and Mary were there with some of Keith's cattle. They weren't alone.

A group of Indians surrounded them. Though Sheriff Doyle felt the desire to go outside and help, he knew there was no hope. The redskins had their weapons ready, giant green bones that were sharpened to points.

"We have to do something," Stacklee said. "Can't we open the windows, shoot some of them?"

Doyle shook his head. "So far, the Indians aren't trying to get in here. Maybe there's a reason for it or maybe not but I don't think we should be attracting attention."

"So we're going to let them die?"

"It's not about that. I'm thinking of me. I'm thinking of you, Betty, Bluford, and this man here." He gestured to Calamaro. "You think he can take another fight? Look at him. His face is practically falling off, for Christ's sake."

Bluford broke his silence. "Can't we do anything?"

"Not if we all want to live," Doyle said. "Okay, well, let's get some water and food ready for when we have to leave."

Silently, the group gathered supplies but no one looked outside as Mary and Keith succumbed to the Indians. After it was done, their corpses were covered in the remains of the tentacled cattle and then set on fire. Blue-green smoke filled the air and sent the stench of musky seawater through the town.

\* \* \*

Betty and Calamaro were filling canteens with water when she said, "You're quiet. What're you thinking about?"

Calamaro shook his head. "I don't know. Maybe it's just all the killing. More killing than I've ever done and it was all in one town."

"You had no choice."

"I know," he said. "But that doesn't make it any easier."

They were silent again as they filled a couple of canteens with whiskey.

Betty said, "Are you going to stay with me when we get to Keoma?"

"I'm not going."

"What?" Betty nearly dropped the whiskey bottle. "Not going? What're you talking about?"

"Before when I said I was staying, I meant for good. Once everything is clear, you all should go but I don't think I'm fit to do any more traveling. At least not for a while."

"So you're just going to stay here? There's going to be no one left!"

"I think a town of ghosts just might be what I need right now," Calamaro said. He finished filling a canteen and then leaned over to kiss Betty. She accepted the soft kiss from those wounded and bloody lips, wishing that she'd have them for a bit longer.

"Then it'll be goodbye for good, huh?" she said.

"I'm afraid so."

"You know you never told me what your daughter's name was."

Calamaro's head came down just a bit. The thought of his child brought heaviness to his heart and mind. "Sara."

"And your wife's?"

"Victoria."

"That's a beautiful name."

Calamaro kissed her again. "So is Betty."

# PART 3
## Exodus of the Damned

# CHAPTER THIRTY-SIX

Sergio led Clayton and Leonard through the desert.

They were fortunate because the Indians didn't see them leave and therefore didn't follow them. Clayton, in particular, took this to mean that they were lucky and vowed to play a dice game in the next town they got to.

As they walked, Sergio kept his eyes forward and never attempted to add to the other men's conversation. He didn't say a word until he stopped next to a tall pink cactus and pointed straight ahead. He said, "Bella...."

Fifty feet away, in a haze of heat and dust, stood his sister, Belladonna Cardinale.

Sergio ran up and wrapped his arms around her. He sobbed on her shoulder, not shy about showing his tears in front of Clayton and Leonard. "Bella, I thought you were dead."

She said, "You came to find me?"

"Yes."

"You found the man who took me?"

"Yes."

Belladonna ran her hand through Sergio's hair. "And you killed him?"

"I had to."

"You know I always hated your killing."

"I know." Sergio let out a deep sob. "But I had to."

"Remember when I was a child and that preacher hurt me?"

"Of course I remember."

"And you hurt him. You hurt him real bad. He couldn't preach anymore. He couldn't see, couldn't speak. Not after you got done with him."

"He deserved it." Sergio gritted his teeth. "He deserved worse."

"So why didn't you kill him, then?" Belladonna said.

"I don't know. Maybe I figured if I killed a man of God, something would happen to you. Now I know the truth."

"The truth?"

"That there is no God that gives a shit about you or me or anyone," Sergio said. "You were nothing but an angel all your life and look what happened to you and for what reason? What's God trying to prove? That good people like you deserve to be tortured by preachers and mayors? It doesn't make a goddamn bit of sense."

"Your anger's going to eat you alive someday." Belladonna kissed her brother on the head and then gently pushed him away. "I have to go now."

"What're you talking about? Go where?"

"I love you, Sergio," Belladonna said. Her body broke into dust and fell to the ground.

"Bella!"

Clayton and Leonard slowly walked to Sergio and put their hands on his shoulders. They said nothing because they didn't think there was anything they could say.

Sergio said, "You saw her, right? I'm not crazy. You saw her?"

Leonard lowered his eyes which were starting to tear.

"Yeah, Sergio," he said. "We saw her."

# CHAPTER THIRTY-SEVEN

Sheriff Doyle stood watch at the front of the brothel while Stacklee took the back. Bluford and Calamaro watched from the upstairs windows.

Slowly, the slaughter in the town decreased and the streets became a cemetery with no crosses. Bodies littered the streets, some dismembered, some on fire, and some intact. Stray Indians still roamed and amused themselves by taking ears, noses, and assholes as trophies.

Then the last of the redskins left in the direction in which they came. Bluford and Calamaro came downstairs.

"Looks like they packed up and left," Bluford said. "I don't see any of them anywhere closer than east on the horizon. You think it's safe to go now?"

Sheriff Doyle said, "Just as long as we travel west and keep an eye out. Could be that they're just playing with us and will come back looking for survivors."

Betty said, "Why didn't they attack us? Looks like they broke into every building, every house but they didn't come in here."

"I don't know and frankly, I don't give a shit just as long as they don't come back."

Stacklee said, "So, we ready?"

Everyone agreed and then Calamaro said, "I'm staying."

"Shit, are you that stupid?" Sheriff Doyle said. "We

193

have a better chance of getting out alive if we're in a group. You stay by yourself here, you're bound to meet up with those redskins or some other tribe that wants to loot the town."

"I'm staying, that's all."

Stacklee walked up to Calamaro, taking him aside. "You know the sheriff's right. It'd be foolish as hell to stay."

"Then call me foolish. I'm staying and I wish you all the best of luck."

"Shit, man." He patted Calamaro on the shoulder. "Thank you for everything."

"You're the one who should be thanked. Betty is lucky to have a man like you working for her."

They shook hands and then the group got ready to leave. Betty and Calamaro exchanged no more words, only another deep kiss.

Bluford approached Calamaro and said, "Thank you for saving my life."

Calamaro nodded.

Doyle said, "We ready?"

They went out the back door, slowly and careful not to make any noise just incase there were still Indians hiding, ready to ambush.

As they walked, Bluford heard a sound coming from the church. "What the hell was that?"

They all listened and heard the same sound.

"Shit," Doyle said. "Let's just go. If anyone's in the church, they can't see us. So let's hurry up. Go!"

The four of them ran through the sand and out of town. Betty looked back at her brothel and let herself cry for her girls one last time.

# CHAPTER THIRTY-EIGHT

In his frenzied escape, Tom Duma thought the church was the only place he'd be safe from the Indians. Though never much of a religious man, he still held the opinion that the church itself would be untouched by the red pagans simply because God himself would protect it.

He went into the church and found it empty except for broken pews and scattered bibles. On the wall behind the altar scrawled in green paint was a scripture verse. Tom walked up to it.

"Gold is the devil with the broadest shoulders," he read. "Jonah 7:25."

He waited a long time while the Indians attacked the town. Then the noise lessened and he knew that they were leaving. He had been spared.

But then the sound of footsteps echoed through the room and a small Indian boy appeared in the doorway. He wore a stove pipe hat made out of cactus needles and human teeth.

Tom Duma turned around. He stared at the boy and said, "This is a place of God. Do you understand that? This is a holy place."

The boy stood silent and held up a pink pistol.

"Your people are more savage than I ever imagined," Tom said. He was about to pick up a bible and hand it to the heathen when a bullet went through his eyeball and out the back of his head. He screamed and put his finger to the wound and thought it felt like the inside of a wet pussy. Then he ran to his left and jumped out of a window, landing in the church graveyard.

A coffin broke Tom's fall. He found himself in an open grave. With his eye bleeding profusely, he stood up and tried to climb out. He was too heavy for the coffin to hold and the wood broke. Tom looked down with his good eye and saw that there was no corpse in the coffin.

There was gold.

Hundreds of gold coins.

For a few seconds, Tom Duma thought himself a rich man. Then the Indian boy appeared above him, grinning and pointing his pink pistol.

A second bullet destroyed Tom's other eye. This time, instead of screaming, he covered his head and whimpered. "Don't break the glass dolls, mother."

The Indian boy put his hand under his hat and pulled out a pink tentacle as long as a bullwhip.

Now blind, Tom didn't see the Indian's new weapon. He only heard the cracking of the whip.

"Oh please, please, please, please spare me! Please!" Tom blubbered but the Indian had no intention of sparing him.

With another crack of the whip, the top of Tom's skull was sliced off, exposing the brain underneath. The Indian jumped down into the grave and finished the killing with a sharpened oyster shell.

Tom Duma's blood and viscera soaked the gold. The Indian boy reached down, picked up a blood drenched coin, and put it into his mouth. His eyes watered in ecstatic joy. The taste of blood and gold was intoxicating.

# CHAPTER THIRTY-NINE

"Hey Sheriff," Bluford said. "I have to tell you something."

"Yeah?"

"Stacklee already knows and maybe Betty, too. I just think I'd feel better if I was honest about it."

Sheriff Doyle shrugged. "So spit it out. What?"

"I'm a cheat," he said. "A card cheat."

The sheriff shook his head.

"Boy, do you think I give a good goddamn about that now?"

Bluford blushed. "What do you mean?"

"We were attacked by Indians for Christ's sake and you're confessing that you're a cheat? You think I'm going to arrest you now?"

"No. I mean, I think it's just my conscience having to be cleared," Bluford said. "And I thought maybe that this whole thing was God's way of punishing me, sending those pagans to attack the town I was in. Maybe I brought it all down on us."

Sheriff Doyle said, "Bluford, you think God really thinks that much of you?"

"What do you mean?"

"You think out of all the people in the world, God's going to put a bull's eye on you just because you've been cheating at some cards or something? If there really is a God, we're all just insects to him, like scorpions. Hell, even lower than scorpions because we can't even sting him. We're like scorpions with no tails. So I assure you he doesn't give a shit about you pocketing some aces in a poker game."

Bluford dropped his head. "Well...."

"Don't worry about it. It doesn't matter now," Doyle said. "In the long run, we're all just insects."

Bluford thought of Lily. It was a strange feeling finding the mutilated body of a woman you had just screwed. He felt uneasy over the fact that he was the last man she had been with. A woman shouldn't die right after being intimate with a stranger. She should die of old age in her own home after being with her husband. The whole thing was heartbreaking.

The group was silent as they walked. Bluford was about to ask Stacklee how it came about that he was working for Betty when he saw something up ahead.

Three men.

He pointed and said, "Look."

The sheriff squinted in the sun. "Don't look like Indians."

"Survivors, then?" Bluford said.

"I don't know. Maybe."

"So let's go see." Bluford walked over. The others reluctantly followed him.

When Bluford got close enough, he recognized the men. He had seen them in Betty's place and talked to the tall one, Sergio. When he got in earshot of the group, Bluford said, "Hey."

Sergio, Clayton, and Leonard looked at him but didn't respond.

When Bluford looked at Sergio's face, he could tell that he made a mistake in approaching them. There were tears in the man's eyes. He looked as if he'd just been through hell, even more hell than a bunch of crazed Indians attacking the town.

The sheriff said, "Who are you?"

He got no response.

Bluford said, "That's Sergio. I talked to him back at Betty's."

Then Sergio and his two partners all looked at the canteens that Bluford and Betty were holding.

Sergio grunted. "Water."

There was even more tension in the air as Sheriff Doyle took a couple of steps to put himself in front of Betty. "Yeah, it's our water."

Clayton drew his pistol. None of the others even saw his hand go for it. He was that fast.

"Hey, hold on a minute," Stacklee said. "No need for the gun. We can give you a sip of water if you need it."

Sheriff Doyle said, "No, Stack. We're not giving them shit."

"Oh?" Clayton cocked his pistol, aiming it at Doyle.

"You heard me." The sheriff drew his gun and aimed it right back at the bastard in the donkey mask. "You want to play bullet for bullet, that it?"

Sergio said, "Hey."

The sheriff moved his eyes and saw that he had another gun aimed at him. What a bitch it would be if he got shot down right after surviving a goddamn Indian attack.

Stacklee pulled his gun out from his waistband and aimed it at Sergio's head.

As they all stood there waiting for someone else to make the first move, Betty said, "You know he's the sheriff, right?"

Sergio let out a grunt that intended to be a laugh. "Sheriff? I just killed your mayor and you think I'd hesitate to kill your sheriff?"

"You killed the mayor?" Betty said. She wasn't upset but it was still shocking to hear that Mayor Douglas was dead and that the man standing in front of her had done it.

"Yeah," Sergio said. His gun hand was as still as stone.

More silence.

Everyone stared at each other. It was as if lifelong enemies were facing each other for the last time despite there being no history between them.

Finally Doyle spoke. "Put your guns down. I won't arrest you."

Clayton chuckled. "You think we're worried about that?"

Leonard said, "Okay. Looks like we got a stalemate here. Two guns against two guns. Do you know how we solve that?" He pulled his gun and pointed it at Stacklee.

Betty stiffened. She was truly scared. The men looked like seasoned killers. Sheriff Doyle, on the other hand, didn't seem as comfortable holding a gun. His hand trembled just enough to make her worry about the outcome.

"You're not getting the water," Doyle said. "Not alive, you're not."

Sergio grunted.

The tension broke.

Gunshots exploded as triggers were pulled.

A bullet hit Stacklee in the shoulder, knocking him down. Another bullet hit Sheriff Doyle in the chest, sending him backward onto a cactus. Bluford and Betty jumped to the ground, hiding behind a small boulder.

Sergio was hit in the gut. He doubled over and squeezed another shot off, hitting the sheriff in the leg.

Clayton's head was blown away. His donkey mask fell off and was now covered with blood and brains. Through the gore, Betty saw a truly handsome face. It was sad that it had belonged to such a bastard.

Though he didn't want to admit it, Leonard knew that his old age had delayed his reflexes. He only managed to get one shot off that hit the Negro in the shoulder before he felt a red hot bullet tear through his stomach. Leonard turned his head to see Betty holding a gun. The bitch had shot him.

Betty said, "Next man that moves gets a bullet."

No one moved.

A few seconds of heavy breathing and bloody groaning and then Sergio slowly raised his gun. He aimed it at Betty.

Before Sergio could get a shot off, another bullet exploded from Betty's gun and his neck exploded.

Leonard shouted. "Sergio!" He was feeling lightheaded and regretted having raised his voice. He would need all the energy he had in order to stay alive. Old age and bullets didn't mix. So he whispered. "Don't kill me."

"I wasn't going to," Betty said.

"Shoot him, Betty," the sheriff said. He was still draped over the cactus like a ragdoll.

"No," she said.

Leonard was fading into death. He saw giant scorpions guarding a fiery gate. They smiled venomous grins, pointing their stingers at him like vicious rapist cocks. Leonard raised his gun. He wanted to blow those ugly bastards away. He wasn't going to Hell without a fight.

Betty watched Leonard's eyes became milky as he raised his gun.

She said, "Don't do it."

Leonard heard only scorpion-babble as aimed his trembling hand.

Stacklee pointed his gun at Leonard and pulled the trigger, killing the delirious old man. He didn't enjoy it but he wasn't about to stand by and let Betty get hurt.

"Hey," Doyle said. His voice was weak.

Stacklee and Betty walked over to him. They started pulling him off the cactus but stopped when Doyle screamed in pain.

"We got to get you off here, sheriff," Stacklee said.

Doyle shook his head. "No, forget it. I'm done."

"No, you're not."

"Yeah, Stack. I am." Sheriff Doyle's body became

limp but his eyes were still open and aware. "Listen. Just wanted to tell you before I go. I never had any hard feelings towards you. Never had a problem with you being a Negro or anything. I just wanted you to know that. I think you're a good man."

"I appreciate that, sheriff." Stacklee unexpectedly felt tears well up in the corners of his eyes. "I think you're a good man, too."

Sheriff Doyle chuckled. "I'm still going to Hell, though."

"Even so, I imagine God won't make it too hot for you." He watched as the sheriff's head turned to the side, his eyes gazing out at the desert. Betty took a step forward and kissed Doyle on the forehead.

The sheriff didn't feel Betty's kiss, however. He was looking at Calamaro who was standing in the dust. Doyle didn't believe it. Hadn't he stayed back in town? Why was he now standing in the desert smiling at him?

The image of Calamaro said, "When you're about to murder a man, what do you look at?" He lifted his hands. "I've asked this question so many times and you know what everyone says? They say they look at the man's hands. You know what I look at?" He pointed to his face. "I look at his eyes."

Then Calamaro burped, scorpions crawling out of his mouth and onto the ground. The sheriff thought that was strange. The scorpions rushed forward until they reached the bottom of the cactus that was holding Doyle. The creatures began to hum.

Sheriff Doyle said, "I don't understand."

The image of Calamaro laughed. "You're not supposed to."

Betty and Stacklee watched the sheriff as he passed away, his eyes still looking into the direction of the empty desert.

"Let's go," Stacklee said. Behind him, Bluford was standing stiff and nervous. All the violence he had witnessed this day was more than he had seen in his whole life.

"Where're we going now?" Bluford said.

"Keoma, maybe. That is, if the Indians didn't go there, too," Stacklee said. He told Bluford to help him take the sheriff off the cactus. Then they started walking off, with Bluford dragging the sheriff's body.

After a few minutes, they saw someone in the distance. It looked like a woman in a dress. Stacklee stopped dragging Doyle and waved his hands. "Holy shit, it's Kimama!"

The Indian walked faster towards them, smiling. When he reached the group, he looked at the sheriff's corpse. He frowned. "Death came."

Stacklee nodded.

Betty said, "Can you help us bury him?"

"I do not have my shovel but I will help." Kimama motioned for them to follow him.

Bluford said, "Can't we bring him to Keoma and have him buried there?"

"You want to explain how he was killed? They're going to know Indians didn't do it. Not like he's all chopped up like the others," Stacklee said.

Bluford nodded.

Kimama led them to a spot between two black boulders. "Here." He started digging a hole with his hands and was soon joined by the others.

When the body was in the ground, Kimama said a traditional prayer from his tribe. He held his hands up and covered his eyes. "Protect this man for he is not really dead but eternal. His spirit is alive. It is death that has died."

Then Stacklee said a short prayer he had learned from the church he went to as a child. "Lord, take the sheriff as your right hand man. He had a good heart even if the devil sometimes covered it with Hell-dirt."

Betty cried while thinking her own prayer.

Bluford wasn't religious and didn't really know the sheriff too well anyway. He just kept his eyes down out of respect. So much death made him rethink his station in life. Being a professional cheat didn't seem like such a productive way of living anymore. He thought that maybe he could learn to be respectable. Maybe Betty would open up a new business and let him work there. He'd have to remember to ask her.

The group said their goodbyes to Kimama and then started off again, hoping to find solace in the town of Keoma.

As she walked, Betty thought of Calamaro, the handsome stranger that had entered her town dragging a wooden donkey behind him. He had saved their lives and there was a chance that she'd never see him again. Betty didn't want that to happen.

Stacklee thought of death. He thought of all those people in town who meet their fates at the hands of those Indians. That was a shitty way to die. But really, was there a good way to die?

Even if you spend your last earthly minutes in the arms of your husband or wife, you're still leaving them for good and who knows for sure where you're headed? Maybe there isn't a Heaven or Hell like they tell you in church. Maybe you end up spending eternity riding on the back of a giant scorpion that keeps going in circles and you can't tell him the right way to go because your mouth is full of dust.

Or maybe you just end up becoming dirt. That's probably more likely. All the dirt in the world is just the millions of people who died. That's why you bury people in the ground so they're closer to what they eventually become.

Stacklee's thoughts were interrupted by Bluford.

"Hey Stack."

"Yeah?"

Bluford lowered his voice so Betty couldn't hear. "What do you think happens to people when they die?"

It was as if the man had read his mind. Stacklee said, "I'm guessing no one knows for sure."

"Yeah, but what do you think?"

"I guess we just rot until we're dirt," Stacklee said.

"That's a gloomy way to look at things, don't you think?"

"Well, if you get a better idea, let me know."

They continued walking through the desert, occasionally talking or stopping to take a drink of water. But they mostly kept silent.

The journey to Keoma seemed to take forever as if the desert expanded its boundaries for the sheer purpose of allowing the three of them to reflect on death. Betty wondered if they'd ever make it. But even if they reached the town, at least she'd have Stacklee by her side and that made life a whole lot easier to endure.

# CHAPTER FORTY

Calamaro felt wary about Betty and the others walking through the desert alone but he hadn't seen any other choice. He just couldn't go with them.

Now the town was empty except for the corpses of the townspeople who hadn't been lucky enough to survive. It was worse than any of the towns he had seen destroyed by the war.

Standing in front of the brothel, Calamaro savored the silence and stillness of the town. Though he would never get over the death of his wife and daughter, he felt good having saved people's lives and killed some evil men. There was now a balance in Calamaro's mind, something that he hadn't felt in a long while.

That peace of mind was interrupted by a voice behind him that said, "Hey."

Calamaro jumped. He turned around and saw the short, bald man standing right behind him. It was the same man he had seen the previous day, the man with the dead, milky eyes.

The Hard Candy Kid.

Flakes of horse flesh covered his clothes and his eyes were even more intense this time.

"Hey," Calamaro said. He was uneasy but hoped it didn't show.

"Never saw the town so quiet. It's beautiful. Like a garden."

Looking out at the corpses of both humans and animals, Calamaro didn't think the word beautiful was appropriate. He said, "The whole town's ruined. Everyone's dead."

"Yeah, I know."

Calamaro said, "I guess every man has a right to his opinion."

"You're right about that." The Hard Candy Kid looked at Calamaro and squinted. He said, "What the hell happened to your face? Indians get to you?"

"No," Calamaro said. "William Lyons did."

"I believe it. The guy's an asshole."

"He's a dead asshole now."

"Good."

The two of them stood silently side by side for a few minutes. There was no sound except for the occasional desert wind that whistled through the rubble of the town and the squeaking of jailhouse door as it balanced on its loose hinges. Then the Kid dug into his pocket and brought out two dark green candy-sticks. He offered one to Calamaro who declined.

The Kid sucked on his candy while the two of them stood in silence again. Finally, he stopped eating and spoke.

"You know what my earliest memory is?" he said, the candy sticking out of the corner of his mouth. "It's of my father making me beat a dog to death. You believe that? Made me beat it to death because it spooked some of his precious horses. I didn't find out till I was a full grown man that a father ain't supposed to do that, you know? A father's supposed to teach his son how to fish and hunt and take care of his family, shit like that. By the time I realized he was wrong, it was too late. I was already a mean little cocksucker."

"Sounds like the man was a bastard," Calamaro said.

"He was. But it wasn't just him. He was the first who was rotten to me and then all the other boys my age were taller so they took to tormenting me. Even the fucking horses seemed to laugh at me. But I showed them all. Sure as shit I did." He spat onto the ground, covering a scorpion in green phlegm. "You know, soon as I grew up, I realized that when I had a pistol I could make anyone do anything I wanted them to. You know why?"

Calamaro shrugged.

"Because all my life people kept doing that to me." The Hard Candy Kid put another stick of candy into his mouth.

Calamaro said, "Guess you had it pretty rough."

The Kid stared at him, grinding his teeth. The candy broke off in his mouth and fell to the ground. "Rough? As rough as I've had it, I've given it back to everyone and anyone. Men, women, children."

"Don't forget horses," Calamaro said. He realized that it was a mistake to say but he knew the man had a particular thing those animals and he couldn't resist.

The Kid cleared his throat and spat out another gob of phlegm. "You getting smart with me?"

Calamaro shrugged.

"Be smart with me all you want, cocksucker. That's not going to make me go away. I didn't just stay in this ruined town to make conversation with you. I'm here because of what you did."

Calamaro said, "And what did I do?"

The Hard Candy Kid stopped sucking on his candy. The silence was abrupt and ominous. Even the squeaking of the jailhouse door stopped. He said, "You killed my brother."

"Your brother?"

"Yeah. My brother Karl," the Kid said. "But I guess you killed quite a few people since you've been here so maybe you don't remember him. He probably didn't seem that important to you but he was to me. He's the only one who ever did a kind deed for me. He's the one who killed my father."

Calamaro said, "I don't remember your brother. You'll have to refresh my memory." He prepared mentally, visualizing his gun hand pulling his pistol out, pointing it at the guy, and pulling the trigger.

"My brother was the one with the purple beard," he said. "You remember now?"

Calamaro indeed remembered the man with the purple

beard, the one who was beating the girl in the hotel. "I remember."

Before Calamaro could make his visualizations materialize into reality, the Hard Candy Kid threw a punch so fast that he didn't know what hit him until he was staring at the sky.

"I'm going to give you the chance to fight back. You understand? That's more than you gave my brother," the Kid said, taking a few steps into the street. "I'm going to walk away and when I turn around, I want you standing up, ready to face me like a man. Can you do that, asshole? Can you do that?"

Calamaro didn't answer. He was already exhausted from the Indian attack and the punch just added to the wear on his body. Rolling over, he got to his knees as the Hard Candy Kid started walking away. When he was on his feet, Calamaro saw that the Kid was fifty yards away, standing on top of a horse carcass, his boots buried in the animal's guts.

"So, Calamaro, you have any more bullets in that strange gun of yours?"

"Only have one left," Calamaro said. "But that's all I need."

The two men locked eyes and stared silently at each other. Their bodies seemed frozen in place. They were two men locked into a situation that had only two possible outcomes and both had to do with death.

The Hard Candy Kid spat onto the dead horse and said, "It all comes down to this."

"Guess so," Calamaro said.

"That all you have to say?"

"Yep."

The Hard Candy Kid pulled his weapon and sent a bullet through Calamaro's gun hand. The Indian attack had been detrimental to his reaction time.

"You stupid son of a bitch," the Kid said.

Calamaro cried out in pain, his fingers mangled from the shot. Another bullet ripped through his right shoulder, causing him to drop to his knees and cover the wound with his left hand.

The Hard Candy Kid snickered and stomped his feet on the horse flesh beneath him. "You dumb fucking piece of shit. You're a stupid asshole just like everyone in this goddamn town. Miserable piece of shit. You stupid son of a bi—"

His sentence was stopped by a burp and a bullet.

The Hard Candy Kid hadn't even seen Calamaro pull his gun with his left hand, let alone aim and shoot it. Though the Kid was fast, he was also too preoccupied with name-calling. He also didn't know that Calamaro often used his left hand to shoot as well as his right.

Blood bubbled out of the Kid's throat and fell onto his shirt. Candy-phlegm oozed from his lips. He dropped to the ground, his head landing on the dead horse's intestines. His mouth opened, letting free his last breaths as he whispered, "Fucking horses…."

The Hard Candy Kid was dead.

\* \* \*

Calamaro sat in the middle of the street, his right hand torn to shreds and his face still leaking fluid. He was convinced he was close to death. Surprisingly, he found that he wasn't afraid at all. He was anxious.

With his left hand he dug into his pants pocket and brought out a faded photograph. It was the first time he looked at it in months and it hadn't changed. His wife in her dress, holding their child. Two beautiful angels. His beautiful angels.

But now where were they?

Betty said they were in Heaven and he hoped she was right. If that was the case, would he really be joining them?

He kissed the photo and slipped it into his shirt, close to his heart. He fell onto his back. Staring at the sky, he saw Victoria's face in the clouds. Then he realized it wasn't a cloud, wasn't Victoria's face.

It was the smoke from a corpse on fire.

## ABOUT THE AUTHOR

Jordan Krall is the author of Piecemeal June and Squid Pulp Blues. His short fiction has appeared in The Magazine of Bizarro Fiction, Furniture Fangs, and the Bradley Sands is a Dick anthology. In addition to writing, he also works as a cowhand for the Dynatox Ranch in Nevada. He lives with his wife, stepdaughter, and son.

# Bizarro books

## CATALOG    SPRING 2009

*Bizarro Books publishes under the following imprints:*

www.rawdogscreamingpress.com

www.eraserheadpress.com

www.afterbirthbooks.com

www.swallowdownpress.com

For all your Bizarro needs visit:

# WWW.BIZARROCENTRAL.COM

Introduce yourselves to the bizarro genre and all of its authors with the Bizarro Starter Kit series. Each volume features short novels and short stories by ten of the leading bizarro authors, designed to give you a perfect sampling of the genre for only $5 plus shipping.

### BB-0X1
### "The Bizarro Starter Kit"
### (Orange)

Featuring D. Harlan Wilson, Carlton Mellick III, Jeremy Robert Johnson, Kevin L Donihe, Gina Ranalli, Andre Duza, Vincent W. Sakowski, Steve Beard, John Edward Lawson, and Bruce Taylor.

**236 pages   $5**

### BB-0X2
### "The Bizarro Starter Kit"
### (Blue)

Featuring Ray Fracalossy, Jeremy C. Shipp, Jordan Krall, Mykle Hansen, Andersen Prunty, Eckhard Gerdes, Bradley Sands, Steve Aylett, Christian TeBordo, and Tony Rauch.

**244 pages   $5**

**BB-001 "The Kafka Effekt" D. Harlan Wilson** - A collection of forty-four irreal short stories loosely written in the vein of Franz Kafka, with more than a pinch of William S. Burroughs sprinkled on top. **211 pages $14**

**BB-002 "Satan Burger" Carlton Mellick III** - The cult novel that put Carlton Mellick III on the map ... Six punks get jobs at a fast food restaurant owned by the devil in a city violently overpopulated by surreal alien cultures. **236 pages $14**

**BB-003 "Some Things Are Better Left Unplugged" Vincent Sakwoski** - Join The Man and his Nemesis, the obese tabby, for a nightmare roller coaster ride into this postmodern fantasy. **152 pages $10**

**BB-004 "Shall We Gather At the Garden?" Kevin L Donihe** - Donihe's Debut novel. Midgets take over the world, The Church of Lionel Richie vs. The Church of the Byrds, plant porn and more! **244 pages $14**

**BB-005 "Razor Wire Pubic Hair" Carlton Mellick III** - A genderless humandildo is purchased by a razor dominatrix and brought into her nightmarish world of bizarre sex and mutilation. **176 pages $11**

**BB-006 "Stranger on the Loose" D. Harlan Wilson** - The fiction of Wilson's 2nd collection is planted in the soil of normalcy, but what grows out of that soil is a dark, witty, otherworldly jungle... **228 pages $14**

**BB-007 "The Baby Jesus Butt Plug" Carlton Mellick III** - Using clones of the Baby Jesus for anal sex will be the hip sex fetish of the future. **92 pages $10**

**BB-008 "Fishyfleshed" Carlton Mellick III** - The world of the past is an illogical flatland lacking in dimension and color, a sick-scape of crispy squid people wandering the desert for no apparent reason. **260 pages $14**

  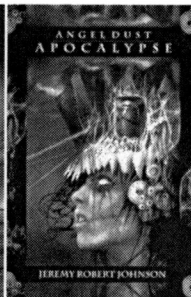 

**BB-009 "Dead Bitch Army" Andre Duza** - Step into a world filled with racist teenagers, cannibals, 100 warped Uncle Sams, automobiles with razor-sharp teeth, living graffiti, and a pissed-off zombie bitch out for revenge. **344 pages $16**

**BB-010 "The Menstruating Mall" Carlton Mellick III** - "The Breakfast Club meets Chopping Mall as directed by David Lynch." - Brian Keene **212 pages $12**

**BB-011 "Angel Dust Apocalypse" Jeremy Robert Johnson** - Meth-heads, man-made monsters, and murderous Neo-Nazis. "Seriously amazing short stories..." - Chuck Palahniuk, author of Fight Club **184 pages $11**

**BB-012 "Ocean of Lard" Kevin L Donihe / Carlton Mellick III** - A parody of those old Choose Your Own Adventure kid's books about some very odd pirates sailing on a sea made of animal fat. **176 pages $12**

   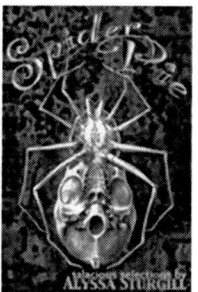

**BB-013 "Last Burn in Hell" John Edward Lawson** - From his lurid angst-affair with a lesbian music diva to his ascendance as unlikely pop icon the one constant for Kenrick Brimley, official state prison gigolo, is he's got no clue what he's doing. **172 pages $14**

**BB-014 "Tangerinephant" Kevin Dole 2** - TV-obsessed aliens have abducted Michael Tangerinephant in this bizarre combination of science fiction, satire, and surrealism. **164 pages $11**

**BB-015 "Foop!" Chris Genoa** - Strange happenings are going on at Dactyl, Inc, the world's first and only time travel tourism company.

"A surreal pie in the face!" - Christopher Moore **300 pages $14**

**BB-016 "Spider Pie" Alyssa Sturgill** - A one-way trip down a rabbit hole inhabited by sexual deviants and friendly monsters, fairytale beginnings and hideous endings. **104 pages $11**

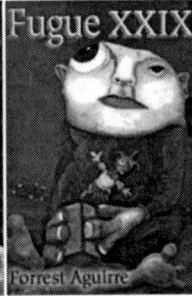

**BB-017 "The Unauthorized Woman" Efrem Emerson** - Enter the world of the inner freak, a landscape populated by the pre-dead and morticioners, by cockroaches and 300-lb robots. **104 pages $11**

**BB-018 "Fugue XXIX" Forrest Aguirre** - Tales from the fringe of speculative literary fiction where innovative minds dream up the future's uncharted territories while mining forgotten treasures of the past. **220 pages $16**

**BB-019 "Pocket Full of Loose Razorblades" John Edward Lawson** - A collection of dark bizarro stories. From a giant rectum to a foot-fungus factory to a girl with a biforked tongue. **190 pages $13**

**BB-020 "Punk Land" Carlton Mellick III** - In the punk version of Heaven, the anarchist utopia is threatened by corporate fascism and only Goblin, Mortician's sperm, and a blue-mohawked female assassin named Shark Girl can stop them. **284 pages $15**

**BB-021 "Pseudo-City" D. Harlan Wilson** - Pseudo-City exposes what waits in the bathroom stall, under the manhole cover and in the corporate boardroom, all in a way that can only be described as mind-bogglingly irreal. **220 pages $16**

**BB-022 "Kafka's Uncle and Other Strange Tales" Bruce Taylor** - Anslenot and his giant tarantula (tormentor? fri-end?) wander a desecrated world in this novel and collection of stories from Mr. Magic Realism Himself. **348 pages $17**

**BB-023 "Sex and Death In Television Town" Carlton Mellick III** - In the old west, a gang of hermaphrodite gunslingers take refuge from a demon plague in Telos: a town where its citizens have televisions instead of heads. **184 pages $12**

**BB-024 "It Came From Below The Belt" Bradley Sands** - What can Grover Goldstein do when his severed, sentient penis forces him to return to high school and help it win the presidential election? **204 pages $13**

BB-025 **"Sick: An Anthology of Illness" John Lawson, editor** - These Sick stories are horrendous and hilarious dissections of creative minds on the scalpel's edge. **296 pages $16**

BB-026 **"Tempting Disaster" John Lawson, editor** - A shocking and alluring anthology from the fringe that examines our culture's obsession with taboos. **260 pages $16**

BB-027 **"Siren Promised" Jeremy Robert Johnson** - Nominated for the Bram Stoker Award. A potent mix of bad drugs, bad dreams, brutal bad guys, and surreal/incredible art by Alan M. Clark. **190 pages $13**

BB-028 **"Chemical Gardens" Gina Ranalli** - Ro and punk band Green is the Enemy find Kreepkins, a surfer-dude warlock, a vengeful demon, and a Metal Priestess in their way as they try to escape an underground nightmare. **188 pages $13**

  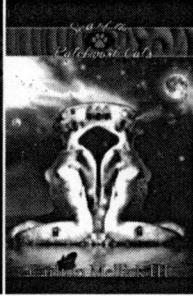 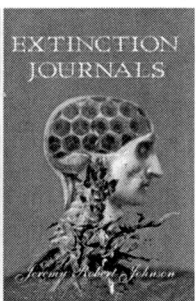

BB-029 **"Jesus Freaks" Andre Duza** - For God so loved the world that he gave his only two begotten sons… and a few million zombies. **400 pages $16**

BB-030 **"Grape City" Kevin L. Donihe** - More Donihe-style comedic bizarro about a demon named Charles who is forced to work a minimum wage job on Earth after Hell goes out of business. **108 pages $10**

BB-031 **"Sea of the Patchwork Cats" Carlton Mellick III** - A quiet dreamlike tale set in the ashes of the human race. For Mellick enthusiasts who also adore The Twilight Zone. **112 pages $10**

BB-032 **"Extinction Journals" Jeremy Robert Johnson** - An uncanny voyage across a newly nuclear America where one man must confront the problems associated with loneliness, insane dieties, radiation, love, and an ever-evolving cockroach suit with a mind of its own. **104 pages $10**

BB-033 **"Meat Puppet Cabaret" Steve Beard** - At last! The secret connection between Jack the Ripper and Princess Diana's death revealed! **240 pages $16 / $30**

BB-034 **"The Greatest Fucking Moment in Sports" Kevin L. Donihe** - In the tradition of the surreal anti-sitcom Get A Life comes a tale of triumph and agape love from the master of comedic bizarro. **108 pages $10**

BB-035 **"The Troublesome Amputee" John Edward Lawson** - Disturbing verse from a man who truly believes nothing is sacred and intends to prove it. **104 pages $9**

BB-036 **"Deity" Vic Mudd** - God (who doesn't like to be called "God") comes down to a typical, suburban, Ohio family for a little vacation—but it doesn't turn out to be as relaxing as He had hoped it would be… **168 pages $12**

BB-037 **"The Haunted Vagina" Carlton Mellick III** - It's difficult to love a woman whose vagina is a gateway to the world of the dead. **132 pages $10**

BB-038 **"Tales from the Vinegar Wasteland" Ray Fracalossy** - Witness: a man is slowly losing his face, a neighbor who periodically screams out for no apparent reason, and a house with a room that doesn't actually exist. **240 pages $14**

BB-039 **"Suicide Girls in the Afterlife" Gina Ranalli** - After Pogue commits suicide, she unexpectedly finds herself an unwilling "guest" at a hotel in the Afterlife, where she meets a group of bizarre characters, including a goth Satan, a hippie Jesus, and an alien-human hybrid. **100 pages $9**

BB-040 **"And Your Point Is?" Steve Aylett** - In this follow-up to LINT multiple authors provide critical commentary and essays about Jeff Lint's mind-bending literature. **104 pages $11**

BB-041 **"Not Quite One of the Boys" Vincent Sakowski** - While drug-dealer Maxi drinks with Dante in purgatory, God and Satan play a little tri-level chess and do a little bargaining over his business partner, Vinnie, who is still left on earth. **220 pages $14**

BB-042 **"Teeth and Tongue Landscape" Carlton Mellick III** - On a planet made out of meat, a socially-obsessive monophobic man tries to find his place amongst the strange creatures and communities that he comes across. **110 pages $10**

BB-043 **"War Slut" Carlton Mellick III** - Part "1984," part "Waiting for Godot," and part action horror video game adaptation of John Carpenter's "The Thing." **116 pages $10**

BB-044 **"All Encompassing Trip" Nicole Del Sesto** - In a world where coffee is no longer available, the only television shows are reality TV re-runs, and the animals are talking back, Nikki, Amber and a singing Coyote in a do-rag are out to restore the light **308 pages $15**

BB-045 **"Dr. Identity" D. Harlan Wilson** - Follow the Dystopian Duo on a killing spree of epic proportions through the irreal postcapitalist city of Bliptown where time ticks sideways, artificial Bug-Eyed Monsters punish citizens for consumer-capitalist lethargy, and ultraviolence is as essential as a daily multivitamin. **208 pages $15**

BB-046 **"The Million-Year Centipede" Eckhard Gerdes** - Wakelin, frontman for 'The Hinge,' wrote a poem so prophetic that to ignore it dooms a person to drown in blood. **130 pages $12**

BB-047 **"Sausagey Santa" Carlton Mellick III** - A bizarro Christmas tale featuring Santa as a piratey mutant with a body made of sausages. 124 pages $10

BB-048 **"Misadventures in a Thumbnail Universe" Vincent Sakowski** - Dive deep into the surreal and satirical realms of neo-classical Blender Fiction, filled with television shoes and flesh-filled skies. **120 pages $10**

BB-049 **"Vacation" Jeremy C. Shipp** - Blueblood Bernard Johnson leaved his boring life behind to go on The Vacation, a year-long corporate sponsored odyssey. But instead of seeing the world, Bernard is captured by terrorists, becomes a key figure in secret drug wars, and, worse, doesn't once miss his secure American Dream. **160 pages $14**

BB-051 **"13 Thorns" Gina Ranalli** - Thirteen tales of twisted, bizarro horror. **240 pages $13**

BB-050 **"Discouraging at Best" John Edward Lawson** - A collection where the absurdity of the mundane expands exponentially creating a tidal wave that sweeps reason away. For those who enjoy satire, bizarro, or a good old-fashioned slap to the senses. **208 pages $15**

BB-052 **"Better Ways of Being Dead" Christian TeBordo** - In this class, the students have to keep one palm down on the table at all times, and listen to lectures about a panda who speaks Chinese. **216 pages $14**

BB-053 **"Ballad of a Slow Poisoner" Andrew Goldfarb** Millford Mutterwurst sat down on a Tuesday to take his afternoon tea, and made the unpleasant discovery that his elbows were becoming flatter. **128 pages $10**

BB-054 **"Wall of Kiss" Gina Ranalli** - A woman... A wall... Sometimes love blooms in the strangest of places. **108 pages $9**

BB-055 **"HELP! A Bear is Eating Me" Mykle Hansen** - The bizarro, heartwarming, magical tale of poor planning, hubris and severe blood loss... **150 pages $11**

BB-056 **"Piecemeal June" Jordan Krall** - A man falls in love with a living sex doll, but with love comes danger when her creator comes after her with crab-squid assassins. **90 pages $9**

BB-057 **"Laredo" Tony Rauch** - Dreamlike, surreal stories by Tony Rauch. **180 pages $12**

BB-058 **"The Overwhelming Urge" Andersen Prunty** - A collection of bizarro tales by Andersen Prunty. **150 pages $11**

BB-059 **"Adolf in Wonderland" Carlton Mellick III** - A dreamlike adventure that takes a young descendant of Adolf Hitler's design and sends him down the rabbit hole into a world of imperfection and disorder. **180 pages $11**

BB-060 **"Super Cell Anemia" Duncan B. Barlow** - "Unrelentingly bizarre and mysterious, unsettling in all the right ways..." - Brian Evenson. **180 pages $12**

BB-061 **"Ultra Fuckers" Carlton Mellick III** - Absurdist suburban horror about a couple who enter an upper middle class gated community but can't find their way out. **108 pages $9**

BB-062 **"House of Houses" Kevin L. Donihe** - An odd man wants to marry his house. Unfortunately, all of the houses in the world collapse at the same time in the Great House Holocaust. Now he must travel to House Heaven to find his departed fiancee. **172 pages $11**

BB-063 **"Necro Sex Machine" Andre Duza** - The Dead Bicth returns in this follow-up to the bizarro zombie epic Dead Bitch Army. **400 pages $16**

BB-064 **"Squid Pulp Blues" Jordan Krall** - In these three bizarro-noir novellas, the reader is thrown into a world of murderers, drugs made from squid parts, deformed gun-toting veterans, and a mischievous apocalyptic donkey. **204 pages $12**

BB-065 **"Jack and Mr. Grin" Andersen Prunty** - "When Mr. Grin calls you can hear a smile in his voice. Not a warm and friendly smile, but the kind that seizes your spine in fear. You don't need to pay your phone bill to hear it. That smile is in every line of Prunty's prose." - Tom Bradley. **208 pages $12**

BB-066 **"Cybernetrix" Carlton Mellick III** - What would you do if your normal everyday world was slowly mutating into the video game world from Tron? **212 pages $12**

BB-067 **"Lemur" Tom Bradley** - Spencer Sproul is a would-be serial-killing bus boy who can't manage to murder, injure, or even scare anybody. However, there are other ways to do damage to far more people and do it legally... **120 pages $12**

BB-068 **"Cocoon of Terror" Jason Earls** - Decapitated corpses...a sculpture of terror...Zelian's masterpiece, his Cocoon of Terror, will trigger a supernatural disaster for everyone on Earth. **196 pages $14**

BB-069 **"Mother Puncher" Gina Ranalli** - The world has become tragically over-populated and now the government strongly opposes procreation. Ed is employed by the government as a mother-puncher. He doesn't relish his job, but he knows it has to be done and he knows he's the best one to do it. **120 pages $9**

BB-070 **"My Landlady the Lobotomist" Eckhard Gerdes** - The brains of past tenants line the shelves of my boarding house, soaking in a mysterious elixir. One more slip-up and the landlady might just add my frontal lobe to her collection. **116 pages $12**

BB-071 **"CPR for Dummies" Mickey Z.** - This hilarious freakshow at the world's end is the fragmented, sobering debut novel by acclaimed nonfiction author Mickey Z. **216 pages $14**

BB-072 **"Zerostrata" Andersen Prunty** - Hansel Nothing lives in a tree house, suffers from memory loss, has a very eccentric family, and falls in love with a woman who runs naked through the woods every night. **144 pages $11**

BB-073 **"The Egg Man" Carlton Mellick III** - It is a world where humans reproduce like insects. Children are the property of corporations, and having an enormous ten-foot brain implanted into your skull is a grotesque sexual fetish. Mellick's industrial urban dystopia is one of his darkest and grittiest to date. **184 pages $11**

BB-074 **"Shark Hunting in Paradise Garden" Cameron Pierce** - A group of strange humanoid religious fanatics travel back in time to the Garden of Eden to discover it is invested with hundreds of giant flying maneating sharks. **150 pages $10**

BB-075 **"Apeshit" Carlton Mellick III** - Friday the 13th meets Visitor Q. Six hipster teens go to a cabin in the woods inhabited by a deformed killer. An incredibly fucked-up parody of B-horror movies with a bizarro slant. **192 pages $12**

BB-076 **"Rampaging Fuckers of Everything on the Crazy Shitting Planet of the Vomit At smosphere" Mykle Hansen** - 3 bizarro satires. Monster Cocks, Journey to the Center of Agnes Cuddlebottom, and Crazy Shitting Planet. **228 pages $12**

BB-077 **"The Kissing Bug" Daniel Scott Buck** - In the tradition of Roald Dahl, Tim Burton, and Edward Gorey, comes this bizarro anti-war children's story about a bohemian conenose kissing bug who falls in love with a human woman. **116 pages $10**

BB-078 **"MachoPoni" Lotus Rose** - It's My Little Pony... *Bizarro* style! A long time ago Poniworld was split in two. On one side of the Jagged Line is the Pastel King-dom, a magical land of music, parties, and positivity. On the other side of the Jagged Line is Dark Kingdom inhabited by an army of undead ponies. **148 pages $11**

BB-079 **"The Faggiest Vampire" Carlton Mellick III** - A Roald Dahl-esque children's story about two faggy vampires who partake in a mustache competition to find out which one is truly the faggiest. **104 pages $10**

BB-080 **"Sky Tongues" Gina Ranalli** - The autobiography of Sky Tongues, the biracial hermaphrodite actress with tongues for fingers. Follow her strange life story as she rises from freak to fame. **204 pages $12**

BB-081 **"Washer Mouth" Kevin L. Donihe** - A washing machine becomes human and pursues his dream of meeting his favorite soap opera star. **244 pages $11**

BB-082 **"Shatnerquake" Jeff Burk** - All of the characters ever played by William Shatner are suddenly sucked into our world. Their mission: hunt down and destroy the real William Shatner. **100 pages   $10**

BB-083 **"The Cannibals of Candyland" Carlton Mellick III** - There exists a race of cannibals that are made of candy. They live in an underground world made out of candy. One man has dedicated his life to killing them all. **170 pages $11**

BB-084 **"Slub Glub in the Weird World of the Weeping Willows"** **Andrew Goldfarb** - The charming tale of a blue glob named Slub Glub who helps the weeping willows whose tears are flooding the earth. There are also hyenas, ghosts, and a voodoo priest   **100 pages $10**

## COMING SOON

"Fistful of Feet" by Jordan Krall
"Ass Goblins of Auschwitz" by Cameron Pierce
"Cursed" by Jeremy C. Shipp
"Warrior Wolf Women of the Wasteland"
by Carlton Mellick III
"The Kobold Wizard's Dildo of Enlightenment +2"
by Carlton Mellick III

# ORDER FORM

| TITLES | QTY | PRICE | TOTAL |
|---|---|---|---|
| | | | |
| | | | |
| | | | |
| | | | |
| | | | |
| | | | |
| | | | |
| | | | |
| | | | |
| | | | |
| | | | |
| | | | |
| | | | |
| | | | |

Please make checks and moneyorders payable to ROSE O'KEEFE / BIZARRO BOOKS in U.S. funds only. Please don't send bad checks! Allow 2-6 weeks for delivery. International orders may take longer. If you'd like to pay online via PAYPAL.COM, send payments to publisher@eraserheadpress.com.

**SHIPPING:** US ORDERS - $2 for the first book, $1 for each additional book. For priority shipping, add an additional $4. INT'L ORDERS - $5 for the first book, $3 for each additional book. Add an additional $5 per book for global priority shipping.

**Send payment to:**

**BIZARRO BOOKS**
 C/O Rose O'Keefe
 205 NE Bryant
 Portland, OR 97211

Address

City                State    Zip

Email                Phone

LaVergne, TN USA
14 July 2010
189485LV00004B/56/P